HARP OF BURMA

HARP OF BURMA

MICHIO TAKEYAMA

Translated by Howard Hibbett

TUTTLE Publishing

Tokyo | Rutland, Vermont | Singapore

Published by Tuttle Publishing, an imprint of Periplus Editions (HK) Ltd.

www.tuttlepublishing.com

Library of Congress Catalog Card Number: 66-20570

ISBN: 978-0-8048-0232-1

Distributed by:

North America, Latin America & Europe
Tuttle Publishing
364 Innovation Drive
North Clarendon, VT 05759-9436 U.S.A.
Tel: 1 (802) 773-8930
Fax: 1 (802) 773-6993
info@tuttlepublishing.com
www.tuttlepublishing.com

Japan
Tuttle Publishing
Yaekari Building, 3rd Floor
5-4-12 Osaki
Shinagawa-ku
Tokyo 141-0032
Tel. (81) 3 5437-0171
Fax. (81) 3 5437-0755
sales@tuttle.co.jp
www.tuttle.co.jp

Asia Pacific
Berkeley Books Pte. Ltd.
61 Tai Seng Avenue, #02-12
Singapore 534167
Tel: (65) 6280-1330
Fax: (65) 6280-6290
inquiries@periplus.com.sg
www.periplus.com

Indonesia
PT Java Books Indonesia
Kawasan Industri Pulogadung
JI. Rawa Gelam IV No. 9
Jakarta 13930
Tel: (62) 21 4682-1088
Fax: (62) 21 461-0206
crm@periplus.co.id
www.periplus.co.id

15 14 13 12　　12 11 10 9 8
Printed in Singapore　　1110MP

TABLE OF CONTENTS

PUBLISHER'S FOREWORD 7

THE SINGING COMPANY 11

THE GREEN PARAKEET 32

THE MONK'S LETTER 89

PUBLISHER'S FOREWORD

Harp of Burma is a story about the Second World War, but its message is a timeless one. First published in 1946, Michio Takeyama's classic tale of a company of Japanese soldiers who faced the trials of war in Burma with a heart full of song has received much acclaim and achieved much renown. It has been produced on the screen and, more recently, has been recreated on the stage. In addition the author received a literary prize offered by the Mainichi Press.

It was for the younger generation that M. Takeyama intended the book, but after its initial publication in *Aka Tombo,* a now defunct but then leading juvenile magazine, it became enormously popular among Japanese adults. It is currently included in a series of recommended world literature classics for high school age youngsters.

On the surface, *Harp of Burma* is the intriguing story of men turned into soldiers, involved in a war they do not fully understand, and faced with experiences both new and baffling. It is filled with adventure, pathos, and humor, all of which go to make a compelling story of war. But, as the author states, he hopes that his readers will not see just another adventurous war story in Burma. "If it succeeds in its goal to set you at least to thinking, then I will be happy," he explains. This edition was prepared for the translations collection of the United Nations Educational, Scientific and Cultural Organization (UNESCO) by Professor Howard Hibbett of the United States.

HARP OF BURMA

Our Japanese soldiers who came back from overseas were a pitiful sight. They looked thin, weak, and exhausted. And some of them were invalids, drained of color and borne on stretchers.

But among the returning soldiers there was one company of cheerful men. They were always singing, even difficult pieces in several parts, and they sang very well. When they disembarked at Yokosuka the people who came to greet them were astonished. Everyone asked if they had received extra rations, since they seemed so happy.

These men had had no extra rations, but had practiced choral singing throughout the Burma campaign. Their captain, a young musician fresh from music school, had enthusiastically taught his soldiers how to sing. It was singing that kept up their morale through boredom or hardship, and that bound them together in friendship and discipline during the long war years. Without it, they would never have come home in remarkably high spirits.

One of these soldiers told me the following tale.

THE SINGING COMPANY

CHAPTER ONE

WE CERTAINLY did sing. Whether we were happy or miserable, we sang. Maybe it's because we were always under the threat of battle, of dying, and felt we wanted to do at least this one thing well as long as we were still alive. Anyway, we sang with all our hearts. And we preferred serious songs, songs with depth, not the frivolous popular kind. Of course most of us had been only farmers or laborers, but we managed to learn some fine choral music.

I still remember with pleasure how we sang on the shore of a certain lake.

We had been on a long march down a valley through dense forests. Suddenly a lake came into view, with white buildings dotting its shore. It was a village where an ancient Burmese king once had a summer palace. Clusters of white-walled houses on a small bay stood half submerged, meeting their reflections in the water. Exotic domes, spires, and bell towers soared into the sky—the dazzling tropical sky.

Have you ever seen an opal? Well, the Burmese sky has just that sort of white glow, tinted here and there with iridescent flecks of light. To see marble towers spiraling up against such a sky makes you feel as if you are dreaming.

During the three days we were stationed in that village we practiced singing every day. We sang hymns, nostalgic old favorites like "The Moon Over the Ruined Castle," pleasant tunes like *Sous les toits de Paris,* and even difficult German and Italian songs. There beside that picturesque lake the captain waved his baton happily, while we soldiers, carried away by the sound of our own voices, sang from the very depths of our beings.

One day we ended by practicing the company song *Hanyu no Yado* over and over again, in four-part harmony. *Hanyu no Yado*—"My Home Sweet Home"—is a song of yearning, one that never fails to stir your heart. As we sang we thought of our families and wished we could show them this landscape and let them hear our song.

Afterward the captain said, "All right, men, that's enough for today. Tomorrow at the same time we'll try something new. Company dismissed!" Then he called to one of the soldiers. "Hey, Mizushima, have you got that accompaniment ready?"

Mizushima was a corporal. He was a lean, sinewy man of medium height, his skin almost black from the sun, and he had big, crystal-clear, deeply recessed eyes. Mizushima had had no musical training before joining our company, but he must have been born with talent since he made such rapid progress. Music was his one passion; he thought of nothing else. He built his own harp to accompany our chorus, and he played so well that he could soon work up an accompaniment to any tune.

It must seem odd that troops in a remote place like Burma would have musical instruments along. But we certainly had them—all kinds of them. If the various instruments belonging to our soldiers were gathered together you would have a really interesting collection. No matter where our troops went, as soon as there was any spare time someone would make an instrument. There were even craftsmen among us who could turn out surprisingly good ones from the most ill-assorted materials. Wind instruments ranged from a simple reed or bamboo pipe with holes bored in it, to a bugle made from parts of broken machinery. As for percussion instruments, I have seen tambourines of cat or dog hide stretched over wooden frames, and even a gasoline drum with one end covered with some kind of skin—a tiger skin, I was told. Anyway, that drum was the pride of its company, and made a tremendous vibrant boom. Some units even had violins and guitars, though it's hard to imagine how they were made.

In our company the instrument we used most was a kind of harp, a copy of the harp that the Burmese play. Its body was made of a thick native bamboo, which was attached to another piece of bamboo, bent and strung with wires of copper, steel, and aluminum or duralumin. Leather thongs were used for the lower notes. After a great deal of hard work we were able to produce a musical scale on this curious harp.

Corporal Mizushima was a master with this harp. He made up all sorts of pieces for it. When he played, tones halfway between a piano and a Japanese lute mingled and hung in the air. At first glance he was a comical sight: a sunburned soldier in a combat cap with his arms around this delicate instrument, playing it as if in a trance.

When Mizushima was asked about his accompaniment to *Hanyu no Yado,* he immediately struck it up. What he played was so elaborate and interesting that it seemed more like a solo piece. The other soldiers gathered around to listen, with arms folded and eyes closed.

The air was heavy and fragrant and very still. The music of the harp traveled out over the lake and echoed back across the water from the edge of the forest on the opposite side. It was a forest of huge teak trees. You could see monkeys frolicking there, and hear all sorts of birds chattering back and forth.

Just at that moment a peacock fluttered down from somewhere, paraded in front of us briefly, and then flapped away. Its wings beat the air noisily, and as it flew, its shadow glided across the surface of the lake.

That is a truly happy memory.

CHAPTER TWO

HOWEVER, the tide of war had begun to turn against us, and at last it was obvious to everyone that our situation was hopeless. We were reduced to fleeing from mountain to mountain through unknown territory, trying somehow to get over the eastern border range into Siam. Once we deliberately chose a steep bypath and spent hours scaling it. Another time we crossed a suspension bridge swaying in the wind over a deep gorge. One by one trucks had broken down, so that we finally had to pull our equipment along in oxcarts, or carry it on our backs. We lived by foraging everywhere we went. It was a wretched time for us, and one of great danger.

We had many harrowing experiences. There were moments when we thought we'd reached the end. But at such times, Corporal Mizushima's harp worked miracles.

One night, high in the mountains, we suddenly found ourselves surrounded by the enemy. They closed in on us gradually and trapped us in a narrow ravine. We had lost our way and could see only by the starlight filtering through the trees above us. We were completely hemmed in.

Enemy troops gathered along the mountain ridges on our right and left and signaled with lights as they searched for us. There was constant gunfire overhead. Shells screeched through the air with a noise like a silk cloth being ripped in two. And just as you thought it was gone, a terrifying explosion would thunder in our narrow little ravine, and rocks and earth would shower down on us.

Thinking we were sure to be wiped out, we huddled together under the trees on the dark, damp floor of the ravine. All of us were prepared to die. We sat there in breathless silence, with our backs hunched, staring wide eyed into the darkness. I could hear my own heart beating wildly, almost in my throat.

The lights on the ridges were flashing signals faster than ever, moving here and there. Then one of our men must have lost his nerve, for a voice at one side muttered: "*Namu Amida Butsu* (Praise the Lord Buddha)."

I heard a sharp reprimanding, "Shh." It was Mizushima. "There may be an enemy scout around here," he whispered.

Everyone was silent again. Once more there was cannon fire overhead; star shells burst so close to us that we were almost blinded; now and then we heard a heavy rain of earth and rocks come pouring down, or a tree trunk splinter.

When that had subsided a little, Mizushima edged up to the captain and whispered something. A few moments later he began climbing up the face of the ravine all alone, carrying his harp. The stars were glittering in the sky; you could see his silhouette among the trees for quite a while, until it disappeared over the ridge.

I'm not sure how much later it was (it seemed like a short time) when we heard twigs crackling in a clump of trees about a dozen yards away. Then we heard someone coming through the underbrush. Two men were talking—in English.

"There's nobody down here," said a strong, young voice. "It must have been an animal."

After a few moments' silence the other one said, "I need a cigarette."

"Too risky!" the first voice warned. "Forget it."

"What do you mean? It's all right—they're not around here."

We heard the scrape of a match and saw a flare of light in that direction. Two British soldiers were sitting on a boulder. The match flame lit up their red cheeks and blue eyes. They were scouts. The match went out immediately. We held our breath and remained motionless. Even in the dark we could see each other distinctly, but the enemy soldiers didn't notice us.

One of them began to whistle softly. The other joined him, humming along in a low voice. It was a tune which we knew as "The Firefly's Glimmer." Presently one of them sighed, and said, "I wonder how my family's getting along."

Just then we heard the sound of a harp coming from the other side of the ridge. At first it was a sad, quiet melody, but soon it became quite passionate, a wild improvisation.

The glowing tip of the cigarette bobbed up in surprise. "What's that?" one of the scouts exclaimed. "Am I hearing things?"

"No, I hear it too. Whoever it is, he really knows how to play!"

We could see the lights on the mountain ridges swarm together for a moment and then head down into the other valley toward the harp.

In the darkness near us the enemy scouts were talking agitatedly.

"Let's go have a look over there—it's probably the Japs."

"Don't be stupid. That must be a native village. But maybe they know where the Japs are." The two soldiers went scrambling up the ridge.

The harp stopped for a while, then started up again even farther away. When one of our men went to investigate he saw that the enemy lights were being lured farther and farther into the distance.

That is how we were saved. Corporal Mizushima returned to us the next morning covered with scratches and bruises.

During our flight we were often attacked by Gurkhas. These ferocious soldiers wore green uniforms and had curved daggers stuck in their leather belts. They would wait in the trees and, as we passed below, sweep us with a sudden burst of automatic rifle fire. We feared the Gurkhas more than anything, and whenever we heard they were in a nearby village we skirted around it to avoid them.

If we came to a forest that seemed dangerous, Corporal Mizushima always changed into Burmese dress and went scouting.

The Burmese look very much like us Japanese, except that they have light beards. However, Mizushima was only twenty-one, and had a light beard and large, clear eyes like a Burmese. His skin was deeply tanned. But above all, though he was a man of great courage and daring, he seemed to have the sad, contemplative expression that tropical peoples such as the Burmese often have, perhaps because of their oppressive climate. And when he wrapped the red and yellow patterned *longyi* around himself he looked just like a native.

He was so convincing in his Burmese outfit that we used to laugh and tell him, "Say, Mizushima, you ought to stay in Burma. They'd love you here."

Mizushima would laugh too, and looking down at himself would put together a few scraps of Burmese. "I . . . native of Burma. Burma is fine country."

Dressed in that disguise he would take his harp and disappear into the forest. If he thought the road was safe, he played the harp and sang a native song. Then the rest of us came out of hiding and made our advance.

Once Mizushima walked right into a band of Gurkhas. In a giant teak tree directly ahead there was a Gurkha astride one of the branches. Biting a red lower lip shaded by a scraggly mustache, the man sat watching him with sharp eyes. As Mizushima took stock of the situation, he noticed more green-uniformed figures here and there in the tall trees, hiding among the leaves.

It was too late to get off the road. Mustering up his courage, he started singing a Burmese priest's song and walked straight under the giant tree.

The Gurkha must have thought he was a traveling musician, for he threw a coin down to him. Four or five other soldiers followed his example and scattered down coins. Mizushima picked them up and bowed his thanks in the traditional Oriental manner, raising the coins to his forehead.

The soldier astride the branch swung his legs idly as he called out in a loud voice, "Hey, seen any Japs?"

Mizushima lifted his arm and pointed to a distant mountain. The Gurkha nodded, drew his curved dagger from his belt, reached out and cut off a fragrant fruit from the tree, and tossed it down to him.

Again Mizushima bowed his thanks. Then, standing under that tree infested with Gurkhas, he played them a tune—a tune we used as a danger signal.

Another time, something rather comical happened. Mizushima had been out scouting so long that we began to worry. Finally, just as we were getting ready to send out a second scout, we heard a faint song—it was our all-clear signal—coming from the depths of the forest.

With a sigh of relief we headed into the forest and found Mizushima crouching in some tall grass, strumming his harp dejectedly. When we came up to him we were startled to see that he was wearing a large banana leaf wrapped around his waist, instead of a *longyi*. The stalk jutted out in the back like a bird's tail feathers.

"What happened to you?" we asked. He explained that a fearsome looking Burmese had jumped out at him from the side of the road and pointed a pistol at his head. It was one of the robbers who were beginning to appear everywhere, using arms abandoned by the Japanese troops. But since most Burmese can be robbed of nothing but their *longyi,* that's what the man asked of Mizushima.

On a scouting mission disguised as a Burmese, Mizushima always went unarmed. To lose his life for the sake of a *longyi* would have meant to fail in his duty, so he did as he was told.

However, the curious thing about these robbers is that they carry a large supply of banana leaves. The Burmese wear nothing under their *longyi,* not even drawers. If you take away their *longyi,* you leave them in a pitifully shameful state; and so the robbers, out of sympathy for their victims, have a subtitute ready to hand over to them. Their language is mild too. Pointing a pistol at you, they say, "Trade me your *longyi* for this banana leaf!"

Burma is a devoutly Buddhist country where the people are content with a very low standard of living. They are a gentle people—without greed, or, to put it less kindly, without ambition. That is one reason why they have lagged behind in the present-day world competition, despite their wealth in natural resources and their high level of education. Brutal criminals never existed in this country. Even these newly armed robbers behaved with the traditional gentleness.

It was lucky for us that the robber had his eyes on Mizushima's *longyi* and not on the harp.

That is how we happened to find Mizushima there in the rank-smelling grass under the scorching sun, naked except for a banana leaf. We went up to him and slapped him on the shoulder saying, "What's the meaning of this getup? Were you bewitched by a fox or something?"

Mizushima gave an embarrassed laugh but returned our teasing. "A banana leaf makes a nice cool outfit," he answered. "Why don't you try it?"

CHAPTER THREE

WE TRAMPED on and on, over mountains, through valleys and forests. We were like the fugitives in the tales of old, frightened even by the sound of the wind.

British forces would parachute down into the villages along our route to block our advance. One village would send word to another about us, and hide their food. Sometimes when we put up in a village for a much-needed rest we would find that the natives had informed the enemy and that we were under attack.

For months on end we were unable to relax our guard. However, a few of the native tribes were friendly, and with their help we made our slow progress over the mountains.

One day we came to a village at the top of a high cliff. Our Burmese guide assured us that we were at last out of danger. He was a tall man and his head was shaved clean—you could see the veins standing out on his scalp. "Look there," he told us, wiping the sweat from his forehead. "You go over that pass. Then you are in Siam."

The vast panorama stretching out before us was really superb. As we stood looking at the view, the cold, bracing air of the mountains swept over us. In the direction the guide was pointing we saw a kind of bluish haze hanging over the dense forest in a sunlit stretch of the mountain range. Beyond that was the Japanese army.

"There are no British or Indian soldiers or Gurkhas around here," the guide said. "Tonight you can have a good sleep."

It certainly looked safe. We were quite a long way from the next village, and the sheer cliff before us dropped off into a deep gorge, where we could see a river with frothing white rapids far below. Behind the village was another high cliff, over which eagles soared in circles. In the center of the village was an open space, and on both sides of that the forest—a dark, fathomless tropical forest. You could hardly imagine a better hiding place for some fifty Japanese soldiers.

The captain said we would stay here for several days, resting and getting ready for the last stage of our march.

As we approached the village, the chief and many of his people came out to greet us. We were ushered to a large thatch-roofed house standing at the edge of the open space. A feast was prepared for us—there was even wine. We were overjoyed.

Until recently the Burmese were so strict in their observance of Buddhist commandments that they never drank alcoholic beverages. Although this custom had begun to break down in the cities, it is still very strong in the country; it was almost impossible to find any liquor along the battle front. But in this case the villagers seemed to have gone to great trouble to get it for us.

They treated us royally. Before we knew it, the feast turned into a lively party, with entertainment. About ten young people from the village stood in a row and sang us one of their folksongs. All of them had kinky hair, and their eyes were brilliantly clear. Yet they were not very dark skinned—we Japanese soldiers were darker. They were barefooted and naked, except for the gay-colored *longyi* wrapped around their hips. At first their song sounded harsh, but when you listened carefully you could hear a plaintive undertone. The song seemed to have no end; just as you thought it was over, it would gather strength again and go on. It was the sad, languid, monotonous music of the tropics.

The guide translated the words for us:

"Far off among the clouds gleam the snows
of the Himalayas—
We bathe in a stream of melted snow.
Far, far off your heart is hidden—
I wish I could bathe my burning heart in that
icy stream."

All through the singing more and more delicacies were served. The ruddy-cheeked, white-bearded chief kept pressing wine on us.

One of our men turned to him and asked: "Can you see the Himalayas from here?"

The chief smiled, and the wrinkles around his eyes deepened. Then, absentmindedly stroking his long beard with both hands, he answered, "They cannot be seen from here. None of us has ever seen them. We only know them through the sutras and our legends."

The Burmese become familiar with sutras and legends in childhood. We often heard the Himalayas mentioned in their songs and stories, and saw paintings or sculptures of these sacred mountains in their temples. They all think of that great mountain range as the home of their soul, and hope to make a pilgrimage to it before they die. People say that those snow-capped peaks among the clouds glow in the sun like marble or beaten silver—a vision of unearthly beauty. And at their foot, thousands of years ago, the lord Gautama meditated on a way to save mankind, and attained Enlightenment. All this is part of the vital faith of the Burmese. Listening with that in mind, we could detect a prayerful quality in their song.

When the villagers finished, we sang. After all, we were the famous "Singing Company." We sang all sorts of songs, but the one most applauded was "The Moon Over the Ruined Castle." That was a real masterpiece. No matter where we went or how primitive the audience, people were enchanted by it.

Drawn by the music, a large crowd of villagers gathered around. The Burmese love festivals. On the slightest occasion they bring out flower-decorated carts and sing and dance. From the time we entered this mountain village the people were in a festive mood, smiling as they vied with one another in devising ways to entertain us. We meant to thank them with our songs.

The villagers listened to us as attentively as if they were at a ceremony. Old people sat in the doorway. Children leaned against the window sills, propping their chins on their hands, and peered in. Under a palm tree in the open place in front of the house squatted women carrying their babies pickaback. All of them were sitting motionless, with their thin arms and legs folded in the peculiar Burmese crouch.

What they liked best was Corporal Mizushima's harp. He sat on a chair with the harp between his knees, playing as passionately as ever. The harp was decorated with orchids and red feathers, and when he plucked the strings vigorously with both hands it made the flowers and feathers dance.

Suddenly, from among the listeners, a young girl stepped forward as lightly as if on air. She was about twelve years old, dressed in a tight-fitting skirt and jacket with curved, winglike ornaments attached at the waist. Her supple arms and legs shone glossily. Her hair was wound in a high, tapering coil, as if she wore a little pagoda on her head.

The young girl stood in the middle of the room, glanced around at her audience, and struck a dance pose. She cocked her head to one side, stretched her left hand out in front of her, fingers straight up, and put her right hand on her breast, palm out turned, forming a circle with her thumb and forefinger. Then, ready to spring into action at any moment, she turned her big black eyes imploringly on the harpist.

Mizushima started to play. The tune was an old school song which he had arranged as a march.

The girl began to dance. Slowly she turned her head from side to side, crossed and recrossed her legs, bent her elbows, her wrists, all her joints, making a series of right angles.

Her slender arms and legs moved with a snaky indolence. Her hands fluttered here and there. She leisurely traced circles with her feet. It was indeed a charming, exotic, unforgettable dance.

The young men of the village shouted her praises and threw flowers at her. They demanded encore after encore. When it was finally over, Mizushima went to a corner of the room and sat on the floor hugging his knees while the villagers cheered.

"How about it, Mizushima?" we asked him. "Wouldn't you like to stay here in Burma and play the harp for the rest of your life?"

Mizushima was always a man of few words, and this time too he only smiled and said nothing. Then he stared straight ahead as if lost in thought.

"Somehow, I like Burma," he used to say. He seemed very much attracted by the tropics—the bright sunshine, the vivid colors, the varied forms of life, the strange customs of the people. He was proud that when he wore a *longyi* he couldn't be distinguished from a native Burmese. And though he was a man who conscientiously carried out his duties, a natural, easy-going life seemed to have a great appeal for him. Whenever we passed a wandering Burmese musician, Mizushima would gaze after him with what was almost a look of envy. When he went scouting he usually disguised himself as a traveling musician. Our teasing about staying in Burma for the rest of his life may have touched him somewhere deep within.

It was time for us to sing again—"The Autumn Moon," "Wild Roses," all lovely melodies we had known since childhood. As we sang, we forgot our troubles. Every one of us had memories linked with these songs. People we loved came to our mind's eye. "Ah, I remember now. Mother was there, and my brothers. . . . I remember how they looked, what they were saying . . ." Such were our thoughts as we sang under circumstances we had never dreamed of, hunted, in peril of our lives, high among the mountains of a strange land.

We sang on and on, each of us pouring our inexpressible feelings into our songs.

CHAPTER FOUR

SUDDENLY we noticed that we were alone. For some reason, all the Burmese had slipped away.

That little girl, the young men—even the chief who had been so busy feeding us was gone. So was our guide, who had promised to arrange for our night's lodgings. We were alone in the house singing to the scattered chairs and remnants of the feast. Even outside, under the windows or in the open space, there were no Burmese to be seen. They had all simply disappeared.

Panic gripped us, and someone shouted, "Stop singing!"

It had often happened that our troops were warmly received in a Burmese village, after which the natives melted out of sight and the enemy attacked from ambush. That was what we seemed to be facing now.

We had to prepare to fight immediately. We had to take up battle positions, put our vital supplies in safe places, find cover for ourselves, dig fox holes. Some of the men started to head for their guns, or rush out of the building.

"Hold it!" the captain ordered. Then, in a low, steady voice, "Go on singing."

After that he began whispering rapidly. "We can't let on we know what's coming. We've got to keep singing as if nothing is wrong—and get ready for them at the same time. It's only been a few minutes since the natives cleared out of here, so the enemy may not attack right away. But once they realize we're digging in, they'll come after us."

We saw that he was right. And we went on singing.

Meanwhile, several of our men crawled across the

floor below the enemy's line of sight to where our weapons had been piled, and brought them back to distribute among us. Singing as calmly and deliberately as we could, we put on our leggings, buckled on our cartridge belts, and took up rifles and ammunition.

We finished "Wild Roses" and began another song. As we sang, we crouched in the shadows and peered through binoculars at the forest. Already we saw a few Gurkhas and turbaned Indian soldiers. You could see them running from cover to cover, scattering among the trees to form a skirmish line. Still singing, we shivered with agitation. Our song was a sad, solemn one, and we sang it as if for the last time. All the while, the captain was busy whispering orders, dividing us into groups of ten, posting us in strategic places.

When the song ended, he ordered, "Clap your hands! Laugh!" We did as we were told, clapping and roaring with laughter.

"We can't tell when they'll open fire," he went on, "but we need every minute they give us. Let's try to keep them off their guard till dark, if possible. Now, once more—laugh!"

We clapped hands again and laughed. But it wasn't easy—after all, machine guns were trained on us from the forest, ready to blaze away at any minute.

Finally, there was only one task left to do, but it was a critically important one. A cart loaded with ammunition cases stood out in the open, and we had to have it safe and close at hand. Furthermore, we had to move it without giving ourselves away to the enemy, though surely they were watching us through their binoculars.

How could we manage that? Still singing, we racked our brains to think of a way. If a single bullet hit that case, we would be finished. Our whole supply of ammunition would explode. We looked at Mizushima, who was good at solving problems like this. He was laughing and singing too, and playing his harp, but we could tell he was thinking as hard as he could. At last he began whispering to the captain.

The trick they agreed on had some of us file out of the house singing a cheerful tune. Mizushima led the parade, playing the harp as he went. The rest followed right behind him carrying flowers that the young men of the village had thrown at the dancing girl. Everyone laughed uproariously, and some even pranced and romped about, imitating a Burmese dance. We lifted Mizushima up on the cart. He stood on the ammunition cases, propped his harp on one knee, and began playing a gay, lively tune. We surrounded the cart, waving the flowers in our hands, and sang in chorus.

Our plan was to draw the cart in as if we were pulling along a festival float. In order to save our breath we picked a slow song—*Hanyu no Yado.*

Apparently the enemy troops had finished deploying, since you couldn't see any movement in the forest. It had become deathly quiet.

We were literally singing for our lives. At any moment there might be a volley of gunfire from the forest. We would have to push the heavy cart as quickly as we could, and yet make it look as if we were doing it for fun. If a bullet flew out of the forest and hit the case it meant certain death—not only for Mizushima, who was standing on it, but for all of us.

The cart began to move. Sometimes we had to clear stones from its path, or heave it up with our shoulders as we pushed it forward. Straining, gasping for breath, still we did our best with *Hanyu no Yado.* On top, Mizushima kept playing his special accompaniment as vigorously as ever. *Hanyu no Yado* is a slow, mournful melody that would touch anyone's heart. Our voices harmonized, low and high parts blending, following, intermingling with one another.

At last the cart had come within four or five yards of our destination.

Suddenly it was night. In the tropics the border between day and night is sharp; as soon as the sun drops below the horizon it becomes pitch-dark. This was an immense advantage to us. All our other preparations were made. Here and there in the shadows little groups of our men crouched with their fingers on their rifle triggers. The captain had his hand on his saber and was staring hard in the direction of the enemy, waiting for the moment to give the command to charge.

Just as the cart reached a safe place, we came to the end of *Hanyu no Yado*.

Instantly the captain drew out his saber. Those of us who had brought the cart stopped singing and took up our rifles. During that brief interval of stillness you could hear, quite distinctly, the river flowing in the valley far below. The birds that had been busily twittering until a few minutes ago were now all fast asleep.

The captain raised his saber. The soldiers were poised, ready to shout their battle cry and charge. But just then the captain checked his command and stood transfixed. An extraordinary thing was happening. Out of the forest soared a voice—a high, clear voice, fervently singing *Hanyu no Yado*.

The captain grabbed one of our men who had started forward, and blocked others by spreading out his arms.

"Wait!" he shouted. "Listen to that!"

The voice in the forest was joined by two or three more, and then by voices from here, there, and everywhere. It was *Hanyu no Yado* sung in English: "Home, home, sweet home . . ."

We looked at each other in astonishment. What could this mean? Weren't the men in the forest the dreaded enemy soldiers who were out to kill us? Were they only the villagers? In that case, we needn't have been so anxious. We gave a sigh of relief and lowered our guns.

Now the forest was full of singing voices. A chorus arose even from the base of the cliff hanging over the river. We joined in and sang too.

The moon was shining. Everything was dyed blue in its cool light. There seemed to be luminous pillars of glass between the trees. One by one, shadowy figures came running out of that forest into the open space.

They were British soldiers.

Gathering into little groups here and there, they sang "Home Sweet Home" with true feeling. We had always thought *Hanyu no Yado* was a Japanese song, but it is actually an old English melody. Englishmen sing it out of nostalgic pride and longing for the joys of their beloved home; whenever they hear it, they think of their childhood, of their mothers, of the places where they grew up. And so they were astonished and moved to hear their enemy—the dangerous enemy they had surrounded high in the mountains of Burma—singing this song.

By this time we were no longer enemies. The battle never began. Before we quite knew what had happened, we were all singing together and coming up to one another to shake hands. Finally we built a bonfire in the middle of the open space and sat around it singing in chorus under the baton of our captain.

A tall Indian soldier pulled out a photograph of his family and gazed at it by the light of the fire. He was a stately, dignified looking man with a white turban and a black beard, but his eyes were as gentle as a lamb's. He showed us the photograph—of his wife and two children smiling under a palm tree. It turned out that he was a businessman from Calcutta.

A soldier whose nationality we couldn't tell asked us to show him our family pictures. One of our men pulled out a picture of his mother; the other soldier looked at it with tears in his eyes.

A ruddy-faced English soldier began to sing "If a body meet a body . . ." He was joined by one of our men, singing in Japanese. Then the Englishman put his arm around our man's shoulder and they strode about together. The Japanese soldier sang at the top of his voice. We all joined in once again.

Mizushima improvised a beautiful accompaniment for this song too. Even the Englishmen applauded him loudly. Looking at the side of his face lit up by the firelight, you could see that tears were streaming down his cheek as he played. There were tears in everyone's eyes as we sang together.

That night we learned that the war had ended three days earlier. Having no way to let their ferocious enemy know, the British troops thought they might have to annihilate us in order to mop up resistance. We threw down our guns.

THE GREEN PARAKEET

CHAPTER ONE

We threw down our guns. From that day we were prisoners of the British forces, something we had never dreamed could happen.

The following night the captain called us together and talked to us. He spoke slowly and haltingly, as we listened in silence.

"We've surrendered," he began. "Not just us but our whole country. I don't know what to think. I don't know what will happen to us, where we'll be taken, or what we'll have to do. I don't even know if we'll be allowed to go on living.

"It's hard to say what condition Japan is in. We lost contact long ago, and since we took to the mountains we've had no way of resuming it. But according to the leaflets and newspapers dropped by enemy planes, our country has been bombed from one end to the other, and many people have been burned, or wounded, or are starving to death. It can't be all propaganda. Our people must be suffering. It makes your heart ache just to think of it.

"Our country is in ruins and here we are, prisoners of war, thousands of miles away. Who could have imagined such a thing? I can hardly believe it's true—the thought of it bewilders me. I ask myself what happened? All I can feel is a sense of shock.

"In time, I suppose the shock will give way to sorrow. We'll probably feel despair, and doubt, even anger and bitterness. But we can't be sure what to think until we learn the facts. Actually, I began to suspect quite a while ago that we might end up like this. But now that it's happened, I have to admit I'm completely at a loss.

"All we can do now is wait to see what the future brings. Our luck has turned against us, there's no use fighting it. If there's no way out, the manly thing to do is to recognize clearly how we stand, accept our lot, and make the best of it. Let's at least have the courage to do that much.

"As far as I know, our situation is hopeless. It looks pretty grim for us. All we have left is our faith in each other. That's the only thing we can count on. It's all we have.

"So let us go on sharing our sorrows and our pain. Let us help each other. Up to now we've faced death together—let's go on that way, sharing the same fate. We have to be ready for hardship. For all we know, we may die here in Burma. If that time comes, let us die together. Meanwhile, let's try not to despair. Let's try to live through this somehow.

"And if the day ever comes when we can go back to Japan, let us go back together—every man of us—and work together to rebuild our country. That's all I can say now."

Our taut nerves slackened, and we sat there in a daze. Everyone stared at the ground, thinking to himself that the captain was right.

I remembered how stirred and excited we had been when we left Japan with cheers ringing in our ears, but how, even so, the whole country already seemed to be in an uneasy mood. Everybody was bragging about our strength, but our words were hollow. We were like drunken bullies. It was a vivid, painful memory, and I burned with shame.

Someone began to sob. Suddenly all the rest of us felt

so sad that we began to weep too. But we weren't sad or bitter about anything in particular. It was just that we felt forlorn and helpless.

Usually we sang when we were unhappy, but that night we didn't. We lay on the floor to sleep, using our packs as pillows. The guns we had guarded so carefully were gone. It was a short, restless night.

After that we spent many unreal days—numb at heart, but frantically busy. Putting our arms and equipment in order, turning them in, transporting them, making various reports and investigations, looking for provisions—all this kept us so rushed that we had no time to think.

When I look back on that period I always recall a certain incident.

The British troops had decided to stay in that village for three or four days, and relegated the menial tasks to us prisoners of war. One morning several of us were on K.P. duty. We were to pluck some chickens the villagers had offered to the troops.

Packed tight in a basket, the chickens stuck their heads out through the meshes and worriedly looked here and there, jerking their cockscombs. A Burmese cook grabbed one bird at a time from the basket, laid it on a stone, and chopped its head off with a *dah*—a hatchet-like implement that the Burmese wear hanging from their waist.

The cook chewed betel nut and spat out red juice as he lazily did his work. Betel nut is the fruit of the betel palm; the people of Southeast Asia chew it like chewing gum, but it is red and dyes the mouth, teeth, and lips an unpleasant color. The cook chopped the heads off one bird after another, and we were to pluck them.

To our astonishment, one of the chickens that had just had its head cut off started to flutter about. Flapping its wings and scattering downy feathers, it hopped around erratically. We were caught by surprise and dropped the chickens in our hands. They came alive too, and stretching their headless necks ran around in circles.

There were about a dozen chicken heads lying strewn on the ground. All of them had a sickly, reproachful look about them with their beaks open and their whitish eyelids closed. But the headless bodies were still alive; they were still flapping their beautiful sleek wings. Drunkenly weaving here and there, the birds finally ran into the bushes, or cowered down in the grass.

Everybody gathered to see this strange sight. There were some who laughed, but others frowned distastefully.

"How do you suppose it feels, running around like that without a head?" someone asked.

At that point the captain came over, looking for Mizushima. "Mizushima, where are you?" he called in a loud voice. Mizushima came on the run.

"We just got an intelligence report," the captain told him. "You see that mountain?" He pointed to a triangular rocky peak in one of the distant ranges. "Some Japanese troops are holed up there, and they won't surrender. For three days now the British have been attacking them, but they're still fighting back. At this rate they'll have to be wiped out. I asked a British officer to let one of us go over and try to talk them into giving themselves up. I told him we want to do what we can to prevent any useless killing, and he said we could try it. How about it, Mizushima, will you go and see if you can persuade them? If you don't, I will."

We all looked toward the triangular peak. It seemed to be about half a day's walk away. It was near the Siamese border, and its gray head jutted out of a thick forest. We strained our ears to listen but could hear no explosion. Thin columns of smoke rose from villages here and there in the valleys below; perhaps it was only our imagination, but the atmosphere near that peak looked yellowish and turbid. There dozens of our fellow countrymen were about to die a useless death. Knowing this, we stared toward the peak.

Mizushima thought for a while and then answered crisply, "I'll go." Then he added, "I don't know how I'll manage it, but I'll do whatever the situation calls for."

"Good," the captain said. "Our company is being sent to a P.O.W. camp in Mudon, in southern Burma. When you've finished your mission, follow us there. The British officer says they'll let you rejoin us."

The two men saluted.

Mizushima got ready right away. He dressed lightly, carried no arms, and wore no insignia. The captain took off his own shoes, which were still in fairly good condition, and insisted on exchanging shoes with him. Then he gripped Mizushima's hand firmly. For our part, we slipped him a broiled chicken leg.

Ten minutes later we saw Mizushima with a British soldier and a guide walking along a path under the cliff far below us. Mizushima had rations strapped to his waist and was carrying the harp on his shoulder. When he looked up and saw us waving our caps, he smiled, raised his hand to the harp, and strummed a loud chord.

As we watched him go, we thought that Mizushima was the kind of man who could carry it off, that his mission would probably be a great success.

CHAPTER TWO

UNDER the orders of the British army, our company went from the mountains into the plains, then by boat down the Sittang River, and at last by train and truck to Mudon. There we were put into a P.O.W. camp.

Our fears for our own lives soon disappeared. We learned that our country had been defeated, almost destroyed, but that it was not entirely ruined and that we prisoners of war were to be repatriated some day.

In Mudon we began our new life of waiting for the day to go home.

Our quarters consisted of a simple *nipah* house—a hut of bamboo poles with the floor high off the ground, topped by a thatched roof. It was too well ventilated to get very damp. We had to sleep without bedding, but that was no real hardship in such a hot climate. The house was enclosed by a bamboo stockade, which not only kept us in but kept others out. An Indian sentry stood at the entrance, and whenever he saw a vendor or anyone trying to steal in, he would fire blank shots to scare him away.

There was a long row of stockades like this, and each of them held a group of prisoners. However, we were forbidden all communication with the other prisoners, so we knew nothing of what was going on outside. Regulations of this kind were strictly enforced, but otherwise the treatment was lenient.

Now and then we would be ordered out on some construction or lumbering job, but on the whole we lived an uneventful, monotonous life, with nothing to do.

We hadn't spent peaceful days like this for a long time—for years, in fact. We had been constantly agitated, harassed, pursued; always tense and anxious about what might happen next. During the past year especially, we lived in a world of blinding flashes and deafening explosions. Suddenly all that stopped—now there were no bombings, no commands, no jumping to our feet in the middle of the night. From one day to the next we stayed quietly in our little *nipah* house, gazing out at a palm grove. At first it seemed almost unbearably strange to us. As we sat there vacantly, we felt nervous and fearful in our hearts. Eventually, though, this vague uneasiness left us and we became used to our quiet life.

But just as we were feeling more relaxed, a different sort of uneasiness began to trouble us. This time we worried because Mizushima had been gone so long.

At the beginning we were confident that Mizushima would join us here in a few days. We expected the gate to swing open any moment, and Mizushima to walk in as vigorous and high spirited as ever. We often found ourselves looking toward the gate. Sometimes we even thought we heard his footsteps.

But no matter how long we waited, he never came.

"I wonder what's happened to Mizushima," we were always saying. "We can't sing well without his harp."

"Not only that, we don't get much work done without him."

"Things seem dull when he isn't around . . ."

Day after day we waited in vain. Mizushima did not return. Whether he actually reached the triangular peak, whether he was able to rescue those die-hards from suicide, we did not know. We had taken it for granted that Mizushima could carry it off. But now we realized what a terrible assignment it was. Quite possibly our own troops would kill him for urging them to surrender.

As the days went by we became more and more impressed with the danger of his mission. We only hoped he might return safely, even if he had failed.

The captain frowned and said, "I can't believe he was killed. There was heavy fighting in that area, so he may have been wounded. Maybe he's getting treatment somewhere. I wish we had a way of finding out—he'd certainly come back as soon as he could, so he must have run into trouble. I hope it wasn't too serious . . ."

We all worried like this, but there was no news of

Mizushima. Everybody kept talking about him; still, since we were prisoners, we could not relieve our anxiety by sending someone out to investigate. Several months went by in this way.

On the days when we had no lumbering or construction work to do, we couldn't help talking about Mizushima. We often spent those days in the palm grove behind the compound, gathering materials to repair our house, which was frequently damaged by typhoons and heavy rains. During a single day in the grove we could gather what we needed for almost any kind of repair. The trunk of the palm tree is long and hard enough to be used for posts or beams; its leaves are good for roofing, and the fibers of its thick coconut husk, which are water resistant, can be twisted into strong, durable rope. With these materials you could easily patch up a simple *nipah* house, no matter how badly damaged it was.

In fact, every part of the palm tree was useful to us. We made all kinds of household necessities from it. The outer husk of the coconut served as a scrub brush; if we split the shell in half, we had two bowls; if we attached a handle to one of them, we had a dipper. You could fashion the hard, round shell into a variety of other things too, or draw out the fibers and make a rough twine, which some of the soldiers wove into baskets and sieves. It was as if kitchen utensils were hanging in a tree. And we bound the leaves to make brooms. A palm tree gains and loses one leaf cluster each month, keeping the number of leaves on the tree constant. In other words, each palm tree sheds one broom a month.

The coconut is famous for its high food value. Inside, it is full of a cool liquid which smells a little green but tastes good. They call this "milk," in English. From the white coconut meat, or copra, an oil is extracted. The oil is made into margarine and soap, among other things. Copra is very nutritious, and can be eaten raw. The natives grate it and eat it sprinkled over other foods, or rolled into a dumpling and baked. You can make sugar by boiling down the sap from the flower stalks. Some kinds of palm trees yield starch from their trunks.

It is even possible to make palm wine. You cut a gash in the flower stalk and fix a bamboo tube under it. As the sap collects in this tube, it ferments naturally and soon turns into a delicious wine. But since the Burmese do not drink wine, we never saw them making any. This method is used in the Dutch East Indies, where many Japanese soldiers learned it and acquired a taste for palm wine. There was a man in our company who loved it so much that he would secretly leave bamboo tubes attached to the trees in the coconut grove. He was delighted whenever a storm blew up. Nothing pleased him more than having a chance to repair the roof.

The palm tree is certainly a priceless treasure. They say that in Europe a farmer who has a cow will never be in want. I suppose the coconut palm is the cow of the tropics.

One day we felled a tree in the grove and were busy making rope, binding and trimming leaves, and boring holes in the coconuts. The soldier who loved wine kept sneaking off somewhere now and then, coming back with a red face cheerfully humming a Burmese song.

Ordinarily, whenever someone started to sing the rest of us would join in. But this time we continued to work in silence. Mizushima used to sing that Burmese song when he went scouting. It was the "all clear" signal.

The drunken soldier was merely humming a tune at random, but to us it sounded as if we were hearing a faraway song, accompanied by a harp, from the depths of the forest. In our mind's eye we saw the forest ahead of us, the birds flying high above, and the *longyi*-clad Mizushima disappearing among the trees.

The captain, who was weaving palm leaves together

to patch a wall, muttered to himself, "I should have gone." He frowned and bit his lip.

Those of us who heard him knew what he meant. He regretted having given his young subordinate such a dangerous mission.

One night there was a terrible storm. Rain fell in torrents, and the palm grove moaned in the wind. Frequently we heard a thud as a coconut dropped to the ground. That noise had started up with the wind, and it went on throughout the night.

We lay in the dark listening, unable to fall asleep.

"There's another one," a soldier grumbled.

"Those damned coconut trees have been dribbling their milk all night long."

Then someone began singing in a low voice:

> "Coconut palm on a lonely island,
> Why don't you go to sleep? . . ."

The wind roared. "Another one!" a man exclaimed, lifting his head. And then, "Ah, that song was a favorite of Mizushima's . . ."

"Quiet!" a voice called out. "We have work to do tomorrow—let's get a little sleep!"

Mizushima was so much on our minds that one day we were really startled. It was about three months after we came to Mudon. Our company had been repairing a bridge at the outskirts of town; a long, crude affair of planks laid side by side spanning several river beds. After working in muddy water for days we had at last finished the job and were crossing the bridge early in the afternoon on our way back to town. Just then we saw a Burmese monk with his skirts tucked up coming toward us.

As we passed him on the bridge we were struck by his resemblance to Mizushima. The monk was still a young man, and his head was shaved clean. He held a begging bowl in his hand and wore a new yellow robe draped loosely from one shoulder, on which perched a bright green parakeet. No doubt he came from a neighboring village.

He was the very image of Mizushima: medium height, well-built, with large, deep-set eyes and tightly drawn lips. And he was darkly sunburned, probably because of his daily begging. With a Japanese army cap on his head he could easily have passed for Mizushima. He seemed embarrassed—and a little angry—because all of us prisoners peered into his face, one after another. Even his serious-minded expression was astonishingly similar.

We had to go in single file along the narrow bridge, and as we squeezed by him, one at a time, we glanced at each other and laughed at the resemblance.

Finally the Burmese monk seemed resigned to our rudeness. Holding the parakeet to his shoulder with one hand, he passed by in silence with downcast eyes.

After crossing the bridge, we turned and saw the monk walking very rapidly along the opposite bank, heading north, away from town. Soon he disappeared into a sparsely wooded grove.

That night we lay on the floor of our hut and talked about the monk.

"Mizushima used to dress like that when he went scouting."

"I'd like to bring him here and give him a harp, and have a concert."

"We'll do that for your funeral."

"Don't be funny . . . but where is Mizushima, anyway?"

CHAPTER THREE

THIS BURMESE monk must have come to Mudon often, since we used to see him from time to time. Whenever we did, we missed Mizushima all the more. One day on our way to a construction job we came face to face with him. One of our men shouted, "Hey, Mizushima!"

The monk stopped, hung his head as if frightened, and waited for us to pass. We felt amused but also rather sad.

"Don't make fun of him," the captain warned. "Look how you've scared the poor man."

Thus we kept on waiting expectantly for Mizushima, but he never came back. We got discouraged, and our miserable life as prisoners seemed even more dreary.

Moreover, we now found ourselves in the long, humid, suffocating rainy season. A steamy vapor-like rain fell for days without a break. Water washed down the roof of our *nipah* house continuously. The grove of palm trees looked blurred, like an ink drawing on wet paper. It was the kind of picture that made you want to take a blotter to it.

We lived in a dull, lethargic reverie. We stopped singing and abandoned our few remaining instruments, letting them slowly deteriorate. Some men just sat hugging their knees and staring up at the sky. Some lay on the floor all day long. Once a man who appeared to be asleep was found crying under his blanket. We even began to quarrel with each other, something we'd never done before.

"Say, what happened to my leftovers?" one of the men demanded, waving his empty mess tin. "I was going to feed it to the monkey myself."

"What are you complaining about? For the last two

days I've been feeding him out of my rations, haven't I?"

The captain was keeping a monkey to cheer us up, but even the monkey became a source of argument.

At last the captain started us singing again, for the sake of our morale. Whenever the rain let up we went out into the yard and practiced. It was such a long time since we'd filled our lungs with fresh air that we felt as if we were coming back to life.

Various activities were beginning in the other stockades too, probably for the same reason. Some put on plays, others went in for sports, a few were even holding classes. As soon as there was a performance of any kind a group of Burmese would gather outside the bamboo fence to watch. Sometimes they clapped their hands enthusiastically, or joined in the laughter.

Our singing was especially popular. We always sang better when we had an audience; we talked about how many people were there, how a certain man had come back a second time, how our singing had won out over a rival play.

All kinds of people from the town gathered at our fence. Since they were tropical people with plenty of time on their hands, they would lean against the fence or the trees and watch from morning till night. They applauded every song. The children learned the tunes and imitated us, forming their own choral group. Sometimes young girls in their gayest red or blue finery danced to our music. That was really delightful. Some of the old people used to wrap up coins and food and toss them over to us on the sly. The guard would pretend not to see them, and would hum along with us when we sang something he knew. But we never sang *Hanyu no Yado*, because it awoke too many painful memories.

One day, when we were in the middle of a song, one of our men nudged another and pointed toward the audience. In the back of the crowd stood a Burmese monk. It was the monk we had seen on the bridge—Mizushima's double. He had the green parakeet on his shoulder and was gazing steadily at us with his deep-set eyes.

When we finished singing we craned our necks to get a look at him.

"You see! He's a dead ringer for Mizushima!"

"No, he's a lot older."

One of the men took a packet of coins that had been tossed in to us and threw it toward the monk. It landed at his feet. A boy picked it up and reverently gave it to him. The monk clasped his hands in a quiet gesture of thanks. It was a priestly gesture, so full of sincerity, that several of us responded by saluting him.

We were much impressed by the way the people of this country respect the priesthood. Their almsgiving is no mere act of charity but one of gratitude to those who do penance for the salvation of all living beings. They don't just hand over their gifts; they kneel and offer them respectfully. We didn't know this at first and must have seemed rude in making our contributions.

After that the monk often came to our stockade. He always stood motionless behind the other spectators as he gazed at us. We used to toss him coins and food that we had been given.

"He's back again!"

"There's always a handout here, so that tramp is making a good thing of it," someone else said scornfully.

"Everybody gets excited about him, but you can see how different he is," said another. "Even if Mizushima was the quiet type, he wasn't a halfwit like this monk. Remember how great he was, standing on the ammunition cart playing the harp?"

That day the monk seemed to have come back from a long journey. His robe was ragged and dirty, his hair was grown out, and his bare feet were bandaged. Because he was a holy man, he was probably always going off on pilgrimages.

The Burmese are so religious that every man spends part of his youth as a monk, devoting himself to ascetic practices. For that reason we saw many young monks of about our own age.

What a difference! In Japan all the young men wore soldiers' uniforms, but in Burma they put on priestly robes. We often argued about this. Compulsory military training or compulsory religious training—which was better? Which was more advanced? As a nation, as human beings, which should we choose?

It was a queer kind of argument that always ended in a stalemate. Briefly, the difference between the two ways of life seemed to be that in a country where young men wear military uniforms the youths of today will doubtless become the efficient, hard-working adults of tomorrow. If work is to be done, uniforms are necessary. On the other hand, priestly robes are meant for a life of quiet worship, not for strenuous work, least of all for war. If a man wears such garments during his youth, he will probably develop a gentle soul in harmony with nature and his fellow man, and will not be inclined to fight and overcome obstacles by his own strength.

In former times we Japanese wore clothes that were like clerical robes, but nowadays we usually wear uniform-like Western clothes. And that is only to be expected, since we have now become one of the most active and efficient nations in the world and our old peaceful, harmonious life is a thing of the past. The basic difference lies in the attitude of a people; whether, like the Burmese, to accept the world as it is, or to try to change it according to one's own designs. Everything hinges on this.

The Burmese, including those who live in cities, still

do not wear Western clothes. They wear their traditional loose-fitting robes. Even statesmen active in world politics dress in their native Burmese costume, to avoid losing popularity at home. That is because the Burmese, unlike the Japanese, have remained unchanged. Instead of wishing to master everything through strength or intellect, they aim for salvation through humility and reliance on a power greater than themselves. Thus they distrust people who wear Western clothes, and whose mental attitude is different from their own.

Our argument tended to boil down to this: it depends on how people choose to live—to try to control nature by their own efforts, or yield to it and merge into a broader, deeper order of being. But which of these attitudes, of these ways of life, is better for the world and for humanity? Which should we choose?

One of the men who scorned the Burmese said: "I've never seen such a weak, lazy people. Everything they have, from electric lights to railroad trains, was manufactured for them by some foreign country. They ought to modernize, take off their *longyi* and put on pants. Even the schools here are only for dramatics or music; there aren't any business or technical schools. They say the level of education is high, but that's compared to the rest of Southeast Asia—all it amounts to are priests teaching the sutras in their temple schools. At this rate the country will go to rack and ruin. No wonder it's a British colony."

Someone objected, saying that exchanging *longyi* for pants wouldn't necessarily bring happiness. "Look at Japan!" he said. "And not only Japan—the whole world is in a mess. When people get conceited and try to impose their will on everything, they're lost. Even if they have a few successes, it's worse in the long run."

"Are you saying it's all right to go on forever being uncivilized, like the Burmese?"

"Uncivilized? Sometimes I think we're not as civilized as they are."

"You're crazy. Do you mean to tell me we're not as civilized as the people of this filthy, backward place, who don't even try to work and educate themselves to stand on their own feet?"

"That's right. We have the tools for civilization, but at heart we're still savages who don't know how to use them. What did we do with these tools but wage a gigantic war, and even come all the way here to invade Burma and cause terrible suffering to its people? Yet they accept it and go on living quietly and peacefully. The Burmese never seem to have committed our stupid blunder of attacking others. You say they're uneducated, but they believe in Buddhism and govern their whole lives by it. They spend part of their youth as monks, and the way of the Buddha becomes second nature to them. That's why their hearts are serene, why they live at peace. Isn't that a far nobler kind of education?"

"But what about the low standard of living? It isn't fit for a human being. In the first place, their kind of Buddhism doesn't make sense. Abandon the world. Put up with your miseries. Don't worry about whether things are getting better or worse, just concentrate on saving your soul—and salvation comes only after you leave the world and enter a new life as a monk. That's what comes of taking the Buddha's words literally, I understand. You get this Hinayana Buddhism in Burma. They all become monks. They're not concerned about the real world. Life on earth seems so insignificant they have no desire to invent new things, and it never occurs to them to try to improve their conditions. They still haven't developed a system that lets everybody live in freedom. Can you call that happiness? At this rate there'll never be any progress."

"The Buddha saw through that kind of happiness and

progress, and what it leads to, thousands of years ago. He taught people to stop clinging desperately to this earthly life, and the Burmese are still faithful to his teaching. If you want a more peaceful, civilized world it'd be a lot better for us to imitate the Burmese, instead of the Burmese imitating us."

"Impossible. In the age of the atom bomb you can't be as easygoing as the Burmese."

"It's exactly because we're in the atomic age that we've got to be calmer and more thoughtful. We'd be better off if we put a dangerous thing like that in the custody of Burmese monks."

We could never come to a clear decision as to which system was better. However, we usually ended up by agreeing that Burmese live every phase of their lives in accordance with a profound teaching, and cannot be considered uncivilized. It's wrong to ridicule them just because they don't have the kind of knowledge we do. They possess something marvelous that we can't even begin to understand. Only, they are at a disadvantage because they are weak and unable to defend themselves against invaders like us. Maybe they should pay more attention to life on earth, not dismiss it as meaningless but set a higher value on it.

So the argument ran. Of course we didn't spend all our time arguing; whenever we could, we went outside to sing.

Once we felt like trying a different sort of tune and picked out a certain Burmese folk song, since it was easy to sing in two parts. It was the one Mizushima used in the forest to signal danger.

As we began practicing it, the Burmese outside the fence seemed overjoyed. Old men and women stood hand in hand, singing together, and children climbed on top of the fence and sang.

The monk was there too. We wanted him to sing along with us, and beckoned eagerly to him. But he only stood there absent mindedly, his eyes half closed. Evidently he didn't care to join in such frivolities.

After a while we no longer paid any special attention to the monk's visits. In the meantime we were told that the Burmese were getting too friendly with us prisoners of war; and another bamboo fence was thrown up inside the older one, further separating us from the spectators. Even if the monk came we couldn't give him alms. Perhaps because of this, he stopped coming altogether.

CHAPTER FOUR

As TIME went on, the suspicion that Mizushima was dead deepened in all our hearts. We stopped talking about him. Everyone carefully avoided the subject. Then an unexpected bit of news reached us, and it seemed more certain than ever that he had died.

The source of this news was an old woman vendor who visited the camp. She used to sell things to Japanese soldiers stationed here in Mudon when they were still at the height of their power. She was the kind of woman called "Grandma" that you often find at military posts. She used to treat the soldiers as if they were her own children, doing their laundry and mending, or inviting them to her home for dinner.

This woman was extremely religious even for a Burmese. Having done a great deal of business with the Japanese army, she must have made lots of money, but she gave all her earnings to the temple and lived in poverty. Though we Japanese soldiers were now prisoners, she often came to help us. She would talk to anybody, waving her brown arms and laughing so gaily that her plump body shook. When we heard her laughter we couldn't help being infected and chuckling to ourselves.

Whenever the old woman came, we would be in high spirits all day long. She was the only person the guards allowed to come and go freely, pretending not to notice.

By now she didn't have much business. All she could do was barter with us. Our clothing and other supplies had been meager from the very beginning, but since we couldn't replace them we had saved as much as possible, carrying it all around on our backs, so we still had quite a few things left.

One day the old woman arrived with a large bundle of merchandise balanced on her head. Grinning broadly to the Indian sentry, she came through the gate. We swarmed around her immediately.

"Say, Grandma, give me a banana for this shirt."

"Yes, sir," she answered in Japanese.

"Grandma, I made this bamboo flute yesterday, and it has a good tone. Let me have some *chandaka* for it." *Chandaka* is a kind of brown sugar hardened into bars.

"All right, *kokan*." *Kokan*—our word for barter—was known even by children in many places overseas. But she could speak Japanese quite fluently, in the Osaka dialect. The soldiers stationed here before must have been from the Osaka region.

"Hey, Grandma, I don't want this monkey I bought last time—how about trading it for some *ngapi?*" *Ngapi* is a salty fish paste which the Burmese use to season food.

"No, no, I won't take him back!" the old woman said. "That monkey is too full of tricks. Anybody else want *ngapi?*"

Finally she began rummaging about in her clothing and pulled out a bird. It was alive. It was a small green parakeet.

The bird sat on the old woman's hand, looked about with round, ringed eyes, and fluttered its wings. Then it made a dry rasping noise, clapping its beak and moving its short black tongue, and screamed a piercing, "Ki! Ki!"

"Well, who wants this parakeet?" Fascinated, we all looked at it.

"You know, you can teach this bird to talk in Burmese, or Japanese, or any language!"

"It's the kind that monk carries around," someone said.

"That's right," said another, putting the bird on his shoulder and studying it closely. "He carries it like this . . ."

That started the old woman off again, talking very rapidly.

"Oh, have you seen that monk too? This is his bird's little brother! My next door neighbor caught both of them. He found a tree where parakeets were nesting, spent a whole day cutting it down, and got five birds. He was so delighted he said they were worth three days' work, and he's been taking a holiday ever since. But just as he caught them the monk came along and asked for directions, so my neighbor prayed for salvation and gave him the greenest one. Since then the monk's been going around with that parakeet on his shoulder. This one is a lighter green but isn't he cute?"

The captain was listening too, and when he learned that the bird was related to the monk's he was so touched he gave her his cigarette case for it.

The parakeet soon became the pet of the company and everyone taught him a few words. He learned quickly. As the old woman said, he learned Burmese and Japanese equally well; it gave you an odd feeling to hear him. One of the men tried very hard to teach him to sing, but without success.

On that same day the old woman told us a rumor about a group of Japanese prisoners who had been brought here from the interior. Their company was said to have entrenched itself in a fortress in a rocky mountain to fight to the death, and to have sustained heavy losses—almost all the survivors were wounded. They really looked pitiful. These men were being cared for in a British hospital in Mudon, but not all of them would recover. Those who had already died were buried in the hospital graveyard, and there were some shockingly young boys among them, the townspeople said.

When we heard this, we all looked at the captain. Only a few units kept on fighting after the war ended, so the one she told us about sounded like the one at that triangular peak.

"Grandma," the captain said to her excitedly, "please find out more about that company, and see if a Japanese soldier didn't come on a mission to it during the battle. If he did, ask what happened to him. Find out all about him—whether he's with them now, whether he was wounded, or taken elsewhere. I'll make it up to you the best way I can."

The old woman nodded.

About ten days later she came back. When we eagerly repeated our question, she told us there had been something like that. It was thanks to the soldier from a different unit that they stopped fighting and were saved from being wiped out. But nobody knows what became of him. He was running around back and forth in the line of fire, and must have died there in the mountains.

The captain seemed staggered by the news. We all groaned. "So he *was* killed!" someone cried.

With trembling hand, the captain wrote a letter to that company asking for all the information they could give him about Mizushima's fate. The old woman promised to deliver it, but the next time she came she said a guard caught her with the letter, scolded her harshly, and warned her she wouldn't be allowed near the prisoners if she did such a thing again. Furthermore, she told us those wounded soldiers had been transferred to another hospital and were no longer in Mudon. That was all we could find out.

However, we knew now that Mizushima had accomplished his mission, and that he was not among the prisoners who were brought here from the triangular peak. Our last faint hope of his survival vanished.

We wished that we could at least have his ashes, or a lock of his hair, but of course that was impossible. No doubt his abandoned corpse was lying in some unknown territory, like those of so many of his young countrymen. Such a thought was hard to bear. All we could do was assume that Mizushima was dead—one of the many who were missing in action. The captain kept talking about various possibilities and about not giving up hope, but he knew that his words were hollow. You could see it in his face.

We were used to disappointment, but this time we were really in despair. Our life as prisoners became sadder than ever. We lived from one dull, weary day to the next, taking each as it came.

Meanwhile the rains ended and we were at last in the dry winter season, but our spirits did not revive. We felt aimless, hopeless, drained of energy. We tasted the full bitterness of being prisoners, unable to control our own lives. Even when we sang together we couldn't feel our old enthusiasm. Probably the Japanese everywhere were in a state of apathy and despondency at that time.

Nobody paid attention to our parakeet any more. Neglected, he would perch on the roof spewing out nasty remarks in Japanese and screeching, "Ki! Ki!" in a rough, piercing voice. But the bird was good at catching mice, and sometimes in the middle of the night he would raise a great racket on one of the crossbeams pecking a mouse to death.

After we had spent over half a year in captivity there was a series of weird, inexplicable incidents, one after the other, until our repatriation to Japan. Baffled, suspicious, and fearful, we talked about them almost every night.

CHAPTER FIVE

In ABOUT the seventh or eighth month of our life as prisoners we started going out regularly on a construction job. We were to repair a building behind the Mudon pagoda. Soon the remains of many dead English soldiers were to be placed in this building, and we had to finish our job by that time.

One day, because a festival was going on, we were allowed to visit the pagoda during our rest period.

The temple compound was full of people. Dressed in bright holiday colors, they crowded together so thickly that you couldn't see where you were going. Pigeons were flying around the golden needle-like spires and curved rooftops, and flowers had been strewn on the stone paths and stairs. But in spite of the large crowd it was very quiet. The Burmese go barefooted, and walk about noiselessly, like shadows.

We took our shoes off too. The worshipers stopped and looked at us. Quietly they drew aside to let us pass, perhaps because they felt sorry for the once-powerful Japanese soldiers.

A boy with clear eyes, curly hair, and glossy brown skin was playing a harp at the foot of a huge open-mouthed stone lion which stood at the temple gate. People tossed coins to him as they went by.

The Burmese harp is a marvelous instrument made of finely polished inlaid wood and shaped like an eggplant. They say that Burmese music began in imitation of the sound of rain drops; anyway, it has a long tradition, and the people of Burma are so fond of music that they have many different instruments and complicated, highly developed melodies.

It used to startle us whenever we heard a harp, because it reminded us of Mizushima. But by now we were accustomed to that, and were neither startled nor saddened. The boy at the foot of the lion played songs that he thought would appeal to the various passers-by. When he saw us he began playing Japanese songs, but we had hardly any money left to give him.

We climbed the stairs and went into the pagoda.

The Burmese make such generous contributions to temples that, although their homes are shabby, their temples are magnificent. Here the great carved marble inner shrine was richly ornamented, and images of the Buddha were everywhere.

Burmese worshipers sat in front of the images with heads bowed and hands joined in earnest prayer. On all sides you could hear voices chanting the sutras. The smoke of burning incense hung in the air. A strangely drowsy, intoxicating feeling pervaded the atmosphere. Most of the worshipers were women who were praying to be reincarnated as men in the next life. They all had long cigars and matches at their knees. In Burma even children smoke, and these women had their cigars beside them so that they could smoke as soon as they finished praying. They don't leave immediately after praying, but sit for hours in a trance as if enjoying the pleasures of paradise.

In one corner a young girl sat on the stone floor holding a pure white lotus blossom between her clasped hands. In front of her against a shadowy wall there was a faintly smiling statue of the Buddha, with a long white arm hanging down from his one bared shoulder. Somehow it looked as if the arm might begin to stir.

Beside her an old man was sitting in a meditative posture. He was sallow and thin, almost a living skeleton. As we looked at him, it dawned on us that he was a leper. We used to stay away from temples because of the many lepers who sat in them to beg or meditate. Seeing that old man made the soles of our bare feet feel itchy.

What a different world! Whenever we saw anything of that kind we wondered how there could be such a country, how people could live such a life.

Still, Japan was probably like that in the old days—it's only during the past eighty years that we've become modern. Because the change has been too rapid it has brought us all sorts of troubles. About the time we were shipped overseas our people were already living in fear and trembling, often going hungry, working like driven slaves. They were pale with worry about the outcome of the war. In contrast, the people of Burma, though gentle and weak and poor, quietly went on enjoying their peaceful, happy lives. They were concerned only with the salvation of their souls.

An English soldier came into the pagoda and looked around curiously. He had taken his shoes off too, following the native custom, but as soon as he noticed the old man he hurried away. As the soldier left, a harp melody wafted in through the door. Apparently the boy at the gate had come nearer. He was playing *Hanyu no Yado*—"Home Sweet Home"—probably to please the Englishman.

Hearing this song so unexpectedly, we were overcome with emotion. It was a long time since we had heard it played on a harp. We all listened with bowed heads. Even the many Buddhist statues facing this way and that seemed to be listening. The soft, quavering music sounded like thin rain falling on tropical flowers. We thought about Mizushima, and prayed to the Buddha that his soul might rest in peace.

Since the harp was outside we couldn't hear it distinctly. But its lingering tones, now high, now low, joined in innumerable intertwining strands, fading in and out like the long sigh of a soul drifting toward heaven.

After a few moments the captain stiffened. "Listen!" he said, straining his ears. Then, excitedly, "Did you hear that chord?"

"What is it, sir?" one of the men asked, looking at the captain's odd expression.

"Shh!" He kept on listening, but the sound of the harp was getting farther away. "Let's go!" he said, and we left the pagoda.

As he walked quickly ahead, the captain emptied his pockets of whatever coins he had and clutched them in his hand. We had to push our way so hastily to keep up with him that people looked at us in astonishment.

At last we caught sight of the boy with the harp standing in the crowd near the gate. The captain went up to him, gave him all his money, and motioned for him to play. The boy stared at him with wide-open eyes, but dutifully took up his harp. The captain began singing *Hanyu no Yado*, and urged him to play it.

Just then we heard a police whistle. The Indian soldier in charge of our company was outside the gate beckoning to us and shouting an order. "Fall in! Your time's up!"

There was nothing we could do about it. Reluctantly the captain led us away. Behind us, as we filed off, we heard the boy playing a Burmese popular song.

That night the captain said, "Where do you suppose that boy learned *Hanyu no Yado?*"

We hesitated, wondering why he was so concerned. Finally one of the men said, "It's a well-known tune, and the Englishmen here are always singing it . . ."

"No, that's not what I mean. It's the way he played it. Didn't it surprise you?"

We tried to remember, but could think of nothing unusual about it.

"That chord, that kind of harmony—would most Burmese play that way?"

"Would they?" we asked ourselves. The only harp version we knew was Mizushima's, and today in the pagoda we had only heard part of a single stanza. With so little to go on, we could hardly even guess.

"Of course every arrangement has its special style," the captain added. "Today I had the feeling I was hearing Mizushima's style. Wasn't it his arrangement? Didn't anybody else think so?"

That startled all of us.

"But, captain, could you tell from so far away?" someone asked.

"Well, maybe not . . ." The captain began to look doubtful. "Maybe it was just my imagination."

Nevertheless, this was such an intriguing notion that we spent the whole night arguing about it.

The captain is a trained musician, it was pointed out, so he ought to be able to tell from even a snatch of music whether or not it was a chord a Burmese would use. You could rely on his ear. But if it was Mizushima's arrangement, where in the world did the boy learn it? Who taught it to him? If we could only get hold of him and ask, maybe we could follow that up and find out something about Mizushima.

Probably Mizushima taught it to someone just before he died. Like the warrior-flutist in one of our old tales, he must have wanted to pass on the secrets of his art before dying in battle. If only we were free, we'd go out and find the boy and ask him how Mizushima died.

Our talk became more and more animated—but then it took a sudden turn.

Would he really have had time to teach his arrangement to anyone? When Mizushima went to that triangular peak the battle was already at its height. As soon as he arrived he must have started "running around back and forth in the line of fire," as the wounded soldiers reported. In that case, he could only have taught it after the company surrendered. It would mean that Mizushima survived the battle, that he was still alive . . .

By this time we were seething with excitement.

Still, when we thought it over, the possibility seemed much too vague. It all depended on whether or not the boy was playing Mizushima's arrangement—but how could we be sure? The captain regarded Mizushima as his own brother and, above all, felt responsible for having sent him to his death. That was why he was so eager to cling to even the faintest hope that Mizushima was alive.

After that we didn't see the boy again. And as the days passed we forgot even that vague possibility.

CHAPTER SIX

Some weeks later, we went to cut trees in a large forest near the pagoda. We were to make lumber for shelves in the mortuary hall where the remains of the English dead would lie in state.

Since it was the dry season with one fine clear day after another, we enjoyed our labor. Everyone worked energetically. At last we were coming out of the apathy and exhaustion caused by the humid weather and the shock of defeat.

When the axe bit into a large tree trunk, wet chips of wood flew like snow. On one side we hewed out a deep wedge, and on the other, a little higher, we made a second cut. Soon the treetop started swaying, and the great tree with its clinging vines and moss began to reel like a living creature. For a moment, as if trying desperately to keep its balance, it hung in the air. But when we gave it a final blow the tree leaned over with a terrible rending sound, and then came crashing thunderously to earth, the heavy trunk snapping from its root. Everyone jumped out of the way. Leaves rained down on our heads, and the birds that had been in the tree flapped up noisily.

Then we started lopping off the branches, as if we were butchering an animal that was still breathing. Glistening dewlike sap rose from the cuts, exhaling a fresh odor.

Whenever we felled a tree our Indian guard praised us. "You Japanese are really good at it," he would say.

Once, after we had finished off an especially large, tough tree, we were resting and wiping the sweat from our bodies. Sunlight filtered down into the forest through the green foliage, and even the breeze seemed to have a greenish tint. Underfoot the thick moss and grass felt as soft as a cushion. It was delightfully secluded and quiet. All we could hear was the sound of water bubbling and trickling somewhere, probably beneath the moss.

By now the Indian guard trusted us so completely that during these rest periods he used to stretch out on a patch of soft, tufted grass, with a moss-covered tree root as a pillow, and take a nap.

That day one of our men noticed a figure in yellow standing in the shade of a tree not far away. It appeared to be a beggar-like Burmese monk in a tattered robe. He kept staring at us for a while, then glanced around nervously and started beckoning. Our man went to see what he wanted.

The monk was short, large boned, and had sinister-looking eyes and dry, chapped lips. His hair was long and shaggy but his face was clean shaven. Squatting in the grass as if to hide himself, he cringed there hesitantly, with a servile grin.

It looked as if he wanted alms, so the soldier gave him what was left of a tin of his own rations. The monk ate, digging the food out with his fingers, but when the other turned to leave, the monk stopped him and said, "How long have you been in this town?"

"Since last September."

"Hmm . . ." The monk thought for a while. "And when are you going back to Japan?"

"I don't know."

"How about it; is it worth going back? What kind of condition is Japan in anyway?" The monk peered at him anxiously out of those reddish, nasty eyes.

It suddenly occurred to our comrade that this monk had been speaking perfect Japanese. And he realized that the short neck and square shoulders, along with the shrewd way of talking, the whole manner, suggested a Japanese tramp. As filthy and unkempt as he was, he had shaved his face clean, no doubt to make himself look as lightly bearded as a native.

"Say, you're Japanese!" our man exclaimed.

"Shh!" The monk lifted his hands as if to stifle the words and glanced around again. "So you just saw through it? A pretty good disguise, huh?"

"How long have you been going around like that?"

"About a year."

"Before the war ended? Were you a soldier?"

"Sure."

"What are you doing a thing like that for?"

"What for? Listen, if I go back to my company I'll get punished. I deserted and fixed myself up this way, and that's how it is—I'm a wandering monk now."

The captain saw them talking and went over. The deserter started to scramble to his feet, but changed his mind and sat down again. When the captain confronted him, he raised his hand to his bare forehead and, still in a sitting position, gave a military salute.

"Well, well, if it isn't the captain!" he said, laughing. "I'm a deserter, sir. I don't want to go back to my unit, so I've turned into a Burmese monk. I just came to see how our troops are doing, not to be thrown into the guardhouse!"

After listening to his story, the captain calmly advised him to return to his company, since desertion was no longer a serious charge. Why not accept his slight punishment bravely, redeem himself, and go back to Japan with all the others, to work together to rebuild the country? What good was it to stay behind alone and spend the rest of his life wandering around as a fraudulent monk?

The captain did his best to convince him, but the man wouldn't listen.

"I don't like any kind of punishment, captain. I'm trying to find some way of sneaking back to Japan—ouch!" He slapped his hand against his neck, where a big mountain leech had fastened on to him.

The forests of Burma are infested with terrible leeches. When we were fleeing through the mountains, they used to torment us. They would even get under our clothes, in spite of our tightly bound sleeves and leggings, and were almost impossible to remove. The sticky, rubbery thing glues itself to you, and can't be crushed no matter how you pinch or squeeze. As soon as you touch it, it sticks to your fingers.

Finally the "monk" picked off the leech and wiped it on the tree beside him.

"But how do you manage to get enough food?" the captain asked.

"Enough food?" He laughed again. "In Burma, as long as you're a monk you don't have to worry. These people are so pious they give you more than you can eat. If I half tried, I wouldn't have to go around looking like such a beggar."

According to this man, there were lots of other deserters. Some of them had lost their homes or families in Japan; others had married Burmese women, or committed some crime that made it impossible for them to live among their own countrymen—and most of these deserters had become monks. The people of Burma take such good care of their clergy that a monk need never starve.

Even so, Japanese long to be with other Japanese. You can't forget your comrades. Living alone among foreigners, you can't help wanting to visit the P.O.W. camp of your old unit. Like a moth drawn to a flame you come to find out when they'll be repatriated, and whether you ought to go back with them too, if you can, or else stay on here in Burma.

This man wanted to find out how his former comrades were getting along, but didn't know where they were. He'd already visited most of the Japanese P.O.W. camps in Burma, and they didn't seem to be in Mudon either. If we went back to Japan he wanted us to let his family know that he was alive. He gave us his hometown address, and asked if we had any men in our company from the same place.

As he spoke, he became quite calm, apparently realizing that the captain was a kindhearted man who had no intention of harming him. By the end he was making his request in the most polite language.

During the deserter's story the captain listened intently, as if fascinated. When the man got up to leave, the captain clasped his hand and said simply, "Take care of yourself."

The deserter's attitude was no longer sullen and belligerent. He bowed deeply and walked away, occasionally looking back at us. At last he disappeared into the forest.

That night in camp we all talked about the meaning of the day's incident. Japanese soldiers become Burmese monks and go visiting P.O.W. camps. In that case . . . maybe the monk who used to stand behind the crowd staring at us with deep-set eyes wasn't just a double.

Maybe he was the real man. But how could that be possible? Mizushima still alive, a deserter, wearing a yellow robe and walking around barefoot, carrying a green parakeet on his shoulder? Yet even though he joined the crowd at our fence he never greeted us. Why? What could his motive have been?

It was so fantastic that none of us knew what to say.

"How about this?" the captain asked. "Suppose Mizushima is alive—do you think he'd have any reason for not wanting to come back to us?"

We all answered that we couldn't believe it.

For the next few days the captain was sunk in thought, and hardly touched his meals. This went on so long that one of our older men couldn't help speaking out.

"Captain," he said, "it's too bad about Mizushima, but you'd better accept the truth. There isn't a chance he's alive. Mizushima died bravely on that peak. He gave his own life to fulfill his mission and save the lives of his countrymen. He made a noble sacrifice. All of us wish he'd survived, so whenever we see anybody who looks like him we get our hopes up—but it's no use.

"When Mizushima put on a *longyi* he looked just like a Burmese, so it's no wonder we see Burmese people who look like him. It's because you believe he's alive that you think they're Mizushima. The sound of a harp reminds you of the way he played. We're grateful that you care so much for your men, but if you ruin your health on account of it the whole company will suffer. Please resign yourself to the fact that there is no hope."

The old timer was earnest and straightforward. As he spoke, he sat stiffly erect in front of the captain, resting one of his big hands over the other on his knees.

The captain nodded. "I suppose you're right," he said, looking very sad. There were tears in the old soldier's eyes too.

CHAPTER SEVEN

AT LAST our work on the mortuary hall was finished, and it was ready to house the remains of the English dead.

For reasons of military strategy the Japanese army had built a railroad through an unmapped mountainous region deep in the interior, to link Burma and Siam, using the labor of a great many British prisoners. They worked under terrible conditions and great pressure of time, but worst of all an epidemic of cholera broke out. There in the primeval forest, with inadequate supplies and facilities, with insufficient help, with no doctors at all, the prisoners died by the thousands. It was indescribably horrible. The dead had been buried crudely, but now their bones were to be sent home and had been brought to this town where they were to be kept temporarily in the mortuary hall. The day had come when the remains were to be transferred there in an elaborate ceremony, and because we had worked on the mortuary hall we were allowed to watch the funeral procession.

At the foot of the road leading up the hill to the pagoda there was a crowded square lined with many little shops and stalls. Dust swirled in the air as merchants of every kind carried on their business, crying their wares noisily on all sides. Vegetables, meat, cakes, flowers, cosmetics —whatever the crowd wanted was on sale. You even saw Japanese army uniforms, insignia, compasses, and the like, all stolen when our soldiers were routed. There were food stands where people stopped to eat; women perched side by side on benches, like birds on a telephone wire, and gossiped as they ate.

Men and women of all classes went by carrying parasols. Slow oxcarts passed too, some drawn by a single ox, others by two or three. The oxen had big black eyes, long curved horns, and curiously thin legs; the carts were typically Burmese, with soaring, upswept lines. There were also some carriages from which ladies of high social position peered out through the windows. These ladies had flowers in their hair and wore golden bracelets and jeweled earrings. But their make-up was unusual—their faces were spotted with patches of yellow powder.

We were lined up along one side of this square. Around noon we caught sight of the approaching British funeral procession. People and carts made way for it. For the time being, the busy traffic stopped.

It was a solemn, resplendent procession.

First of all came the mounted police in full dress, riding up at a trot to direct traffic. The police were usually all smiles, but today they looked grave, and wore their chin straps tight. The horses had sleek, well-groomed coats, under which their muscles rippled smoothy. As they trotted nimbly here and there they seemed to be aware of the importance of this ceremony, even to be pleased by their own skill at controlling traffic.

Then the main procession arrived. At its head marched an honor guard of about company strength. The men carried their rifles upside down on their shoulders. They were all strikingly ruddy and held their chests high; their well-fitting uniforms seemed molded to their bodies. They looked like expensive dolls on display. The precision of their marching legs made you think of a pair of combs swinging alternately back and forth.

Next came a group of army chaplains, each with a silver cross hanging at the breast of his black robe. Some were quite aged and dignified looking, their hair as silvery as their crosses.

Behind them followed a number of handsome funeral carriages drawn by elephants. Each elephant bore a kind of howdah on his back; and on the howdah, which was covered with a beautiful rug, sat a turbaned rider deftly handling a slender whip. The elephants had small, prayerful eyes, and coiled and stretched their trunks, breathing with an asthmatic wheeze, as they plodded quietly along. Their massive gray-wrinkled bodies were draped with ornaments, and passed before our eyes like so many moving walls.

The funeral carriages were splendid vehicles of teak or ebony, each laden with floral wreaths and blanketed with a British flag. As they went slowly and sedately by, in utter silence, we stood with our arms raised in a salute. The men lying in those carriages had fallen in a foreign land and were now being escorted faithfully to their eternal rest. We watched the procession reverently.

There was an honor guard behind the carriages too. These were Scottish soldiers in their strange uniforms with tasseled caps and short, boldly striped skirts that left their knees bare. Then came various kinds of military and civilian personnel. Among them was a group of young women who appeared to be nurses. They looked like well-bred ladies of firm character and strong religious conviction.

Last of all were the Burmese. They wore ceremonial dress—long, neatly wrapped *longyi,* with cloth wound around their heads. They included both government officials and monks, and among the latter were some of high rank as well as the ordinary monks we always saw walking in the streets. In Burma, when a person dies, the number of monks in his funeral procession is equal to the number of years he lived. Obviously this time there weren't enough monks to equal the total ages of the dead, although there were a great many.

As we were watching the procession, we were surprised once again. Wasn't that the monk who resembled Mizushima? He was walking along calmly with his gaze fixed straight before him. He had on a bright yellow robe, and his head was clean shaven. Though still young, he appeared to hold a fairly high rank. He had much more dignity than at the time we first met him there on the bridge, along with an air of sadness. Certainly he looked like Mizushima. But his expression was entirely different from that of our lively, fearless comrade. Mizushima's face had hard, determined lines, while this man's face was much softer and had a look of peaceful resignation.

That was only to be expected, of course, but there was one thing that distinguished this monk from all the others. He was carrying a square box wrapped in white cloth; the box was suspended from his neck, and as he walked he held it in both hands, exactly the way the Japanese bear the ashes of the dead. None of the others was carrying such a box.

That day the monk didn't have his parakeet on his shoulder, but as he passed in front of us he lowered his gaze, the way he always did.

"Ah!" the captain exclaimed softly.

Forgetting that we were supposed to be standing at attention, we stared openmouthed at the monk.

He looked like Mizushima, yet different. He looked Japanese, yet like a Burmese. He looked like all the other Burmese monks in the procession, but he was the only one carrying a box. Before long we lost sight of him. More Burmese came by, then a group of oxcarts loaded with offerings, and finally beggars looking for alms. Thus the solemn, magnificent procession ended.

The crowds along the road broke up, and the square became a gay, noisy market place again. Soon you could see the procession going into the temple compound on the hilltop.

Back at camp, we spent another night arguing.

"What did I tell you? It *was* Mizushima!" some insisted hotly. "He's alive after all. He deserted and became a monk."

"But why would he desert, of all men?" others asked.

"Who knows?" No one could answer that.

Some were equally emphatic that Mizushima was dead. "How could that have been Mizushima? You're out of your minds—he's dead! He's been missing almost a year, and those wounded soldiers said he didn't have a chance."

"But what about that chord the captain heard?"

"Well, how do you know it was . . . "

For those who held out that the monk was Mizushima, the strongest evidence was the box he carried hanging from his neck. "Only a Japanese would do that," they said. "When we were leaving Japan we saw lots of boxes of ashes of the war dead, coming home that way. In fact, we've been seeing them for years—those sad-looking boxes wrapped in white hanging from the neck of a soldier just back from overseas, or a grieving father, or even a little son. That proves the monk is Japanese. Who ever saw a foreigner carrying such a thing?"

Those who disagreed said, "What kind of proof is that? Suppose he *is* Japanese, what would he be doing at a British funeral? Why would he carry that box? He could hardly be carrying the ashes of a British soldier in a Japanese box! Didn't you see those beautiful hearses drawn by elephants? And what makes you so sure the box was Japanese? Even the Burmese must use square boxes, and maybe they wrap them in white cloth sometimes, and hang them from their necks. There's nothing wrong with that! Just because a man who looks like Mizushima was carrying a box that looks Japanese is no reason to get so excited, is it? You act as if you saw a ghost!"

At last one of the skeptics said exasperatedly, "We've all gone half-crazy from the war—we're babbling like hysterical old women! Let's cut out this weak-minded, superstitious talk!" His voice rose in anger, but it was sorrowful too. "It's an insult to Mizushima to be squabbling about whether or not he's dead, when he gave his life heroically for his fellow countrymen. He'd never be such a coward—deserting, and tramping around as a monk!"

That night the captain only listened, without offering opinion.

CHAPTER EIGHT

The next day, however, the captain started acting strangely. He retrieved the green parakeet from somewhere and trained him to perch on his shoulder. The bird had been neglected for such a long time that his plumage was dull.

"There, there," the captain said, stroking his feathers. "It's too bad nobody's been looking after you, but I'll take good care of you from now on. And you must learn to speak Japanese for me."

The parakeet shivered as if overjoyed. He snapped his hard beak together several times, and darted his cold, black, rubbery tongue at the captain's hand.

After that the captain shared all his meals with the bird. "Hey, Mizushima!" he would say, and when the parakeet repeated it the captain fed him rice out of the palm of his hand.

Then he would say, "Let's go back to Japan . . ." When the bird repeated that, the captain gave him some meat. And then, ". . . together!" The captain gave him a bit of his *ngapi*. Then he had the bird say it all in one sentence.

He kept this up for about ten days, until finally the parakeet shrieked the words out in a piercing voice as soon as the captain opened his mess tin.

No one could imagine why the captain was doing this. Whenever he started in we looked at each other anxiously, wondering if he might be on the verge of a nervous breakdown from his grief over Mizushima. Anyway, we felt a helpless sadness, mingled with annoyance, when the bird roused us in the middle of the night screeching, "Hey, Mizushima! Hey, Mizushima! Let's go back to Japan together!"

At last the old timer spoke out with blunt sincerity. "Captain," he said, "what good does it do teaching the bird to talk that way? No matter how bad you feel about Mizushima's death you shouldn't give in like that. You sent him on his mission, but that doesn't mean you ordered him to die. After succeeding so well, Mizushima must be satisfied that he didn't die in vain. But if you keep on grieving, and the bird keeps calling for him day and night, it'll ruin our morale. Morale means a lot in this miserable P.O.W. life—when everybody is so anxious to go home they're apt to get depressed. So please try to keep your spirits up, sir."

For a moment there was a painful silence. Then the captain answered hesitantly:

"It may seem foolish, but I still can't give up hope. Somehow or other I want to learn the truth about that monk. If he isn't Mizushima, that's that. But I can't rest without knowing.

"The trouble is, I have no way to get in touch with him, so even though it's unreliable I'm thinking of trying this parakeet. How else can I send a message? I've already trained the bird enough, and now I'd like to have him say those words in the monk's ear the next time we catch sight of him. The two birds are brothers, so ours ought to fly over to the other one. I'm sorry to disturb you all, but I hope you'll put up with it a little longer until we find out if the plan will work."

That's the captain for you, we thought, and we started taking turns feeding the bird and teaching him more things to say.

However, the old timer kept worrying about the captain and glaring angrily at the bird. Then he would shake his head and heave a sigh.

Even earlier, though, the captain had been doing his utmost to get news of Mizushima, but had always failed. Long ago he had explained the whole matter to the British officer in charge of the camp, and asked if he could find out anything about him. The officer was very sympathetic and made a number of inquiries, but without success. The British troops that fought in the battle of the triangular peak had already gone home. The wounded Japanese prisoners had been sent elsewhere from Mudon, and then assigned to various hospitals according to their condition. No one knew where they were. Even if we had known, it would have been impossible for a P.O.W. to go to investigate. All the British army could tell us was that circumstances indicated the man had died.

Then the captain had written another letter, intending to have it delivered to the monk. It said in part: "If you *are* Mizushima, please come back to us—you don't know how much we miss you. Whatever problem may make it hard for you to return, it will be solved. I guarantee that. At least tell us why you're going around in disguise."

Shortly after the funeral procession, before the parakeet had been trained, the old woman vendor came to see us. The captain handed her his letter and asked her to give it to the monk with the green parakeet. But she hastily flung it away, as if it burned her fingers.

"Oh, no! Never!" she cried out. "I wouldn't carry another letter if the Lord Buddha himself asked me!" Having been so severely reprimanded before, the old woman would not listen.

Since he couldn't persuade her to take the letter, the captain asked her to find out who the monk was. But she refused to do even that. The captain talked as persuasively as he could; then he gave her his watch, saying it was for her son. At last she reluctantly agreed to see what she could learn.

"Find out when he first came to this town," the captain said. "Ask if he plays the harp, and what kind of box he had hanging from his neck in the funeral procession the other day."

The old woman listened dubiously, standing with arms akimbo, her clenched fists against her thick hips, and soon got disgusted. "That's ridiculous!" she said scornfully. "What do you want to ask questions like that for? Burma is full of monks. They go traveling here and there, and an awful lot of them play harps, and it's nobody's business what they hang around their necks! Instead of worrying about crazy things like that, you Japanese soldiers ought to be more religious!"

"Yes, we know, Grandma," he said, "but please find out for us anyway."

"If that monk is a good man, we'll study under him and be more religious."

After some further urging, she agreed to try.

While waiting for her to return, the captain became so impatient that he appealed to the British officer for another investigation. But this time the Englishman refused to consider it, because our captain's story seemed so fantastic.

At first the heavy, broad-shouldered Englishman sank down into his chair and listened kindly, but before long a doubtful look came into his blue eyes, and his blond mustache began to twitch. Then he burst out laughing.

"A few harp notes drifting on the breeze—and you believe a dead man's alive! That's interesting, really quite poetic. You must be dreaming."

There was nothing the captain could say.

Around the time the parakeet was thoroughly trained

the old woman came back again. As usual she rambled on and on in a loud voice and couldn't get to the point. But the captain kept pressing her for information, and finally she gave us the following report:

"Well, now, that monk is a wonderful man. He's no ordinary monk. He's a very holy man. At any temple he goes to, people give him the place of honor and make offerings to him. He must have studied terribly hard ever since he was a little boy! He wears a special arm band, you know, and that means he's an outstanding monk—he has the title of Master, no matter where he goes. That band is a little tin strip engraved with a passage from the holy sutras, and it's fastened onto his arm with a cord. Only a very learned or virtuous monk, or one who's done some specially fine deed, can wear a band like that. When other monks see it, they bow and give way.

"And about that box hanging from his neck, the one you were all worried over—well, I asked another monk what was in it, and he got so curious he picked it up once, on the sly, and found it was very light. They say there's a big ruby inside it. Some of the other monks were talking about that, and said Burma is famous for its rubies, but you hardly ever see such a marvelous one, so huge and fiery red. They thought he must have meant to offer it in memory of those dead British soldiers.

"Anyhow, he's only a young man, but he's the kind of monk that makes you feel so thankful you want to cry. Now and then he turns up here in Mudon, but they say he spends most of his time hurrying around the country, going up mountains and down valleys, holding services all over."

Then the old woman muttered to herself what sounded like something from the sutras.

She had shattered our last hope. Such an exalted monk couldn't possibly be one of our deserters. Furthermore, if that box contained a ruby it had no relation to Japanese custom, and it certainly didn't prove that the monk was Japanese, in spite of the way he carried it. All of us who had been clinging to the faint hope that Mizushima was alive gave up completely. We had thought of asking the old woman to put the parakeet on the monk's shoulder, now that it was trained, but we gave that up too.

That night, when we were opening our mess tins, the parakeet heard the clatter and shrieked out from a beam overhead, "Hey, Mizushima! Let's go back to Japan together!"

One of the men looked up and said, "Quiet! We don't even know when *we're* going back to Japan, let alone Mizushima."

The captain seemed despondent. No doubt the strain of prolonged hardship was beginning to tell on him; he had trouble sleeping and was tense and edgy, as if in pain. The old timer did his best to cheer him up.

The old soldier turned the parakeet loose in the forest, but the bird soon came back to us, with bedraggled plumage, and took up its usual perch on our roof.

CHAPTER NINE

THE MEMORIAL service for the English dead continued with great ceremony for days. During that time we were allowed to rest, but once it was over we went to the mortuary hall again to put everything back in order.

The hall was a large one, full of the racks that we had made. The funerary urns rested side by side in endless rows on the tiers of shelving. We heard that these were only a fraction of the whole, but even so the number of urns was astonishing. The sight reminded me of the rows of silkworm cocoons shelved all the way up the walls in a Japanese farmhouse.

We bowed respectfully. All of these men whose bones

were lying here had had their families, their jobs, their hopes. They died in the unknown mountains of Burma from exhaustion or the cruel plague. But fortunately they were now being cared for with reverent dignity. Though only their bones remained, they would soon be able to go home to sleep in peace in the soil of their native land. That was a consolation. If their white bones had been left abandoned in the wilds of Burma, far from friends and relatives, their souls would have been in anguish. Then we who were living could never have forgiven ourselves. We were glad to have made some contribution toward the funeral.

We had escaped with our lives. We were prisoners, but we had never experienced the horrors that these men had known. In time, we could go home and work again. As we stood there with bowed heads, we felt deeply moved by the sufferings of the dead.

We finished our silent prayer and were walking around in the building, when suddenly the old timer exclaimed, "Look! It's over there!"

On the lowest tier in a dark corner at the base of a pillar we saw a square box. It was wrapped in white cloth.

If this had been a Japanese mortuary hall, anyone would have thought that box held the ashes of a dead soldier. But for some reason it held a large red ruby. When the captain saw the box, he gave a cry of astonishment, and then sighed and stood there with outstretched hands as if in a daze. We wondered what was wrong with him. Presently he straightened up to a rigid position of attention, and saluted.

Lately the captain's behavior had been hard to understand. That day the old timer frowned with annoyance and hurried us out of the building, as if to shield us from such a disgraceful sight.

On our way we turned to look back at that simple,

unadorned box, humble and unobtrusive in the corner.

Then we went into a clearing in the nearby forest and sat down. The captain was still behaving strangely. His face was lighted up, and for once he seemed happy. He even kept talking to himself cheerfully. We could hear him say, "Yes, yes, of course!" Then he would laugh, clap his hands together, and gaze up at the clouds in the sky.

"Take a look at that," one of the men said, poking a friend with his elbow. "Maybe the captain's having a nervous breakdown after all."

"Maybe," his friend agreed. "He's practically dancing for joy."

It was hot. The air was heavy and languid. Everything in the tropics is intensely bright, and stays that way with unvarying monotony throughout the year. You feel as if time would flow on like this forever. As usual, the sun was shining; and the brilliance of the red canna lilies in the shadeless clearing almost hurt our eyes.

Before us was an immense statue of a reclining Buddha, and behind that a wall-like cliff. A dense forest surrounded us, and trees overhung the Buddha. Birds were singing in the trees, and monkeys leaping from branch to branch. It was a typically Burmese scene.

Images of the Buddha in this country are very different from those in Japan. Reclining figures are numerous, some of them fifty or sixty feet high where the upper part of the body is half erect. Their heads are small, the lines of their bodies soft and flowing, and they seem neither wholly male nor female. Since the face and body are painted in vivid colors, the skin a creamy white, it looks as if a giant in make-up is lying there alive before you. Confronting one of these figures for any length of time is likely to unnerve a person who isn't used to them.

And there in the shadow of the rock cliff, under a tangle of ivy and banyan roots, a huge, faintly smiling Buddha stared at us with glassy eyes.

To our surprise, the captain jumped up briskly and said, "Well, how about a song?" It had been a long time since he had suggested anything like that. We began to sing.

Once we were singing we forgot ourselves. Our voices came echoing and re-echoing back from the rock cliff, enveloping the Buddha in song. He seemed to be listening attentively, his body half raised.

After we had been singing for a while we noticed a beautiful sound blending with our chorus. We couldn't tell where it came from. It seemed to fall from the high treetops around us, or perhaps well up from the earth. It was the sound of a harp exactly like the harp of our lost comrade!

As we sang we looked around in bewilderment. But the captain seemed more and more elated, and went on leading us vigorously. It became a contest between the harp and the chorus.

Not far away there was a pagoda. Its many small curved roofs were piled one over another, like upturned fish scales. From the end of each of these scales a bell dangled. At first we thought the sound came from the tinkling of the bells, but there wasn't a breath of wind. The more we listened the more it sounded like the harp we had last heard almost a year ago, when we were fleeing across the mountains.

After our song ended, the harp music soared up for a moment and then stopped. Its lingering tones slowly died away, sinking lower and lower as if they were being sucked into the earth beneath our feet.

That great white Buddha lying before us—the echoes of the harp seemed to hover around his smiling lips and then subside into his body.

Everyone ran to look for the harpist. The old timer went around behind the Buddha and into the trees. Just then, with a loud beating of wings, a peacock came flying out of a thicket. For a moment it flew along unhurriedly close to the ground, drooping its lovely tail feathers, but at last it lighted on the Buddha's back. The old timer followed it with his eyes, and yelled, "Hey, there's a door here!"

We all went over and saw that there was an entrance at the back of the great Buddha. Apparently its body was hollow, and you could go inside. Around the entrance was a low archway, leading down a few steps to a door. The archway was made of large bricks which had been plastered over and gilded, but the gold paint had peeled off except for a few traces here and there. From ceiling to floor its walls were choked with the clinging, tangled roots of the banyan tree.

The door was rusty and wouldn't open. It looked as if it had been that way for years—at least, there was no sign that anyone had gone inside the Buddha through this entrance in recent times. And yet the sound of the harp must have come from there. We beat on the iron door until our fists ached.

At this point our Indian guard came running up, shouting angrily for us to get back to work. We had forgotten all about that. We didn't return to camp till late evening.

That night we were sitting around gloomily, without even having our usual argument.

"I wonder if that was Mizushima's ghost!" someone said.

"Don't be stupid."

We fell silent again.

The captain was alone in a corner, playing a rundown guitar. Now and then he would close his eyes, nod happily, and murmur, "Yes, this was the chord. This was how he used to play it."

The old timer caught the parakeet on the roof and brought him in, stroking his feathers as he gazed at him. One of the younger soldiers went over and fed the bird a morsel of meat left from his dinner. "Hey, Mizushima!" he said to him.

The parakeet shook his feathers, shrieked a couple of times, and cried in a hoarse voice, "Hey, Mizushima!"

The old timer put some bread crumbs in the palm of his hand and said, "Let's go back . . ."

The parakeet answered falteringly, "Let's go back . . ."

We all joined in, ". . . to Japan together!"

Somehow the bird managed to blurt out, " . . . to Japan together!"

The parakeet had not forgotten. Everyone took turns training him. Finally he seemed to have had enough to eat, and refused to say another word. But by then he was completely re-trained.

The old timer sat up straight, put the parakeet on his shoulder, and folded his big arms. "Now, how can we get this bird to the monk?" he muttered thoughtfully.

Just then one of our men came bursting into the hut, yelling at the top of his lungs. "We're going home! All P.O.W.'s in Mudon are going home! We leave in five days!"

Everybody jumped to his feet. Some men cheered. The parakeet flapped up from the old timer's shoulder to a beam overhead.

"Are you sure?"

"Of course I'm sure! Let's start packing!"

"There isn't anything to pack!"

CHAPTER TEN

THE OLD woman came early the next morning.

"Congratulations, congratulations!" she said, smiling as she dried her tears. "It really makes me feel happy too. Now you can go home and live a good life. You've had such a terrible time so far."

"Thanks, Grandma. We'll never forget your kindness. When I get home I'll tell my mother all about you."

Each of the men gave her one of the few things he had left, as a souvenir. Finally we handed her the parakeet, and begged her to look for that monk and put the bird on his shoulder. "Tell him we're leaving for Japan in four days. It's the last thing we'll ever ask of you!"

For a moment the old woman hesitated, but then she agreed to do it as a parting favor. Nestling the parakeet against her cheek, she said: "All right, don't worry. I'll see that he gets it. Well, little birdie, you're going to sit on the monk's shoulder and serve the Lord Buddha along with your brother."

She kept saying good-by to us over and over. As sorry as we were to see her go, we were anxious to have her start looking for the monk right away. At last the old woman said, "Well, I'll come back once more before you leave." Lifting her basket to her head, she started to waddle off.

We shook our heads doubtfully as we watched her go.

"She's a good old lady, but you can't count on her," somebody said glumly.

From the next day on we spent most of our time singing in the camp yard, looking over the fence for the monk with the green parakeet. We sang at the top of our voices, late into the evening, hoping he would be lured back by our singing. If he really was Mizushima he'd be sure to come, we thought.

On the first day there was no one remotely like him in the crowd around the fence. Once during the second day someone said, "He's here!" But it turned out to be a different, younger monk.

That night we had another discussion. We were to leave the day after next. We asked ourselves if we didn't have some way to find out, but we only kept going around in circles, repeating the same old arguments.

"If Mizushima doesn't come tomorrow he'll be left behind. He'll never be able to go back to Japan."

"Maybe that monk wasn't Mizushima after all."

"I guess not. You remember what the captain told us the night after the armistice, about sharing the same fate. 'Let's live or die together,' he said. 'And if we go back to Japan, let's go back together—every man of us—and work to rebuild our country.' That's what he said, didn't he? Mizushima was the most determined of all—if he hasn't come back, he's dead!"

"Yes, but that must have been his harp we heard coming out of the Buddha."

"But even the boy at the temple played that way. And why would he come so close and still not join us? . . . Oh, let's forget it."

"What do you suppose *really* happened to him?"

Meanwhile the captain was quietly taking care of the paper work connected with our repatriation. He never mentioned Mizushima any more—he even seemed to avoid the subject. Perhaps he had finally given him up for dead, or succeeded in forgetting him. His attitude had changed somehow, and it bothered us.

By the third day our voices were hoarse. The music sounded anything but beautiful—we were forcing our aching throats. The audience seemed puzzled. And we kept stretching up to peer over the fence so often that everyone wondered what was going on, and turned to look. Those who thought we were staring at them glanced around in bewilderment; children stopped singing with us; young girls stopped dancing and shyly slipped away behind the crowd.

That was how the morning went by.

Burmese monks live by their begging bowls. In the morning they leave their monasteries and come single file to town. The women of every household start cooking before dawn and wait for them. Without a word, a monk stops in a doorway, and a woman reaches out and reverently fills his bowl. Monks eat one meal a day, always before noon. This rule is still very strictly observed. As a result it was shortly past noon, after they had finished begging, that most of the monks came to listen to us.

We kept on singing even during our lunch, and as we sang we could see the monks begin to appear beyond the fence. An old gray-haired monk, so bent his hands almost touched the ground, sat down facing us and started chanting a sutra in a loud voice. Perhaps he thought our songs were hymns to the Buddha, or that we sounded like a choir of angels floating on a cloud in paradise. He was attended by two dark-skinned little boys who stood respectfully behind him holding flowers.

The crowd that day was so large it even attracted professional entertainers. Not far from the fence there was a snake charmer with two cobras. Cobras like music and will do all kinds of tricks to it. These two cobras formed letters on the ground, twined together in various patterns, or separated, lifted their flat heads (from which the fangs had been removed), puffed out their throats, and performed a clumsy dance in time to their master's flute and gong.

Under a nearby tree the boy from the temple was playing his harp. If he had only come earlier, when we could have heard more clearly . . . We felt especially disappointed because he must have been the harpist inside that reclining Buddha. However, the crowd today was listening to our chorus, and he played so little that we couldn't tell anything about his music.

During the past three days we had sung all the songs we knew, except for *Hanyu no Yado*. Each song had its special memories, and now that we were leaving we sang all of them with deep emotion. But the one that moved us the most was *Miyako no Sora*—"The Sky over the Capital."

Miyako no Sora is the school song of the First High School of Tokyo, the one its students sang in farewell to classmates who had to leave to go to war. One after another they went away, as if beckoned by some great invisible hand, and it seems that for a time the song echoed through the school grounds, morning and night. We learned it from an alumnus of this school, when his company happened to be stationed in the same town that we were. It was a fine tune for sending off young men, a tune with a bright, gay rhythm and yet a poignant sadness to it. Even now I can hear it whenever I close my eyes. As I listen, it awakens vivid memories of those days. If the Japanese people had sung more fine songs like *Miyako no Sora* during the war, instead of cheap patriotic songs, everyone might have survived with greater dignity.

That day we sang *Miyako no Sora* as if to lament our tragic youth and, at the same time, we felt consoled; we felt a strength awakening in us. But just as we paused before launching into the climax, we swallowed our voices. Our song was suddenly broken off.

While we were singing, the crowd beyond the fence had shifted—and we caught a glimpse of a man in a yellow robe. We stared at him so hard that some young girls nearby looked embarrassed. Blushing and exchanging shy glances, they edged away.

As the crowd thinned around him, you could see that it was the monk. He had a gleaming green parakeet on each shoulder.

Our performance was over. The people who had been leaning against the fence began to stir. Sensing that something unusual was going on, they looked around curiously. At last they all fixed their eyes on the monk.

But the monk stood as if rooted to the ground, without any change in his expression. Then one of the parakeets stretched itself up and gave a loud, shrill whisper into his ear, "Hey, Mizushima! Hey, Mizushima! Let's go back to Japan together!"

We could hear it distinctly. But still the monk didn't make the least movement.

Was it Mizushima—or wasn't it? We all marveled at the resemblance. The monk gazed steadily at us out of eyes set deep in the masklike face of a mystic. He was not sunburned as we had thought—he even looked rather wan and pallid—and his lips were stained red with betel nut. Draped in a loose robe, he seemed as calm as a statue. His face was the image of Mizushima's, but its expression was softer, gentler. He seemed to be meditating, peering into his own heart.

"Hey, Mizushima . . ." one of our men called in an uncertain voice.

The monk seemed not to hear him. But the lighter of the two parakeets screeched excitedly, and began to cry out again, "Let's go back! Let's go back to Japan together!"

"I guess he's the wrong man," someone said quietly.

The monk stood gazing at us through half-closed eyes. We hesitated. If we had the wrong man we would be insulting a highly revered Buddhist monk, which would also offend the people gathered to hear us. The guard was watching too. There seemed to be no solution, especially since we were separated from him by a double fence.

We whispered together for a moment, and decided to sing *Hanyu no Yado,* Mizushima's favorite. We would be singing it for the first time in many months. As we began, we remembered that happy chorus beside the lake, that dangerous harp accompaniment on top of the ammunition cart. . . . All our feelings of comradeship, the joys and sorrows we had experienced in this strange tropical land, the risks we took, our hopes and disappointments, the drastic change in our fortunes—all this was bound up with the song.

The monk stood there unmoved, as if insensible, yet with great dignity. We sang stanza after stanza, raising our voices high in this final song. Suddenly the monk let his head droop forward. Gathering up the skirts of his robe, he hurried through the crowd toward the boy under the tree. He took the boy's harp, came back to the fence, and raised the harp to his shoulder. Then he launched vigorously into Mizushima's arrangement of *Hanyu no Yado*.

So he *was* Mizushima! We gave a whoop of joy. After such a long time apart, after more than a year, we joined our hoarse voices to his accompaniment. By now he had changed back entirely to the old Mizushima. His mouth drawn tight, his piercing eyes fixed high, he played the harp with effortless abandon.

It was Mizushima through and through! This was Corporal Mizushima, the pride of our company, the man who ranged over the mountains and valleys of Burma with the harp on his shoulder, saving us time and again, pulling us through, keeping our spirits up! We stamped the ground out of sheer joy.

When the song ended, we ran to the inner fence and leaned over it, shouting to him.

"Mizushima, we leave for Japan tomorrow!"

"It's a good thing you finally got back!"

"Hurry up and come in!"

And there were some who called out angrily, almost with tears in their voices. "Where've you been all this time? Explain yourself!"

But Mizushima stayed on the other side of the fence, standing quietly with downcast eyes. After a while he took up the harp again and started to play.

It was a slow, sad tune that sounded oddly familiar . . . of course! It was the graduation song we had all sung on the last day of elementary school. He played it through with beautiful harmonies, and then repeated the refrain: "Now we must part, we must part. . . ."

We listened with aching hearts. Mizushima played the refrain three times, made a low bow toward us, turned quickly, and walked away through the crowd.

Seeing him leave, we all waved our arms and shouted to try to stop him. "Hey, Mizushima! Let's go back to Japan together!"

But the monk only shook his head slightly and went on without a backward glance. Over his left shoulder he carried the harp, with one of the green parakeets perched on it; the other parakeet was on his bare right shoulder. The two birds were chattering away at each other.

THE MONK'S LETTER

CHAPTER ONE

THAT was how Mizushima left us. He revealed himself for only a moment and then disappeared. We never saw him again. He is still there in Burma, dressed as a monk, still wandering about in that land of endless summer.

Mizushima, of all men, was a deserter. He would not come back—that was a cruel blow to us. He had ignored what the captain said after the armistice, had betrayed his friends, abandoned his company, even abandoned his native land. Today Japan is a poor, wretched country which the Japanese themselves vie with one another in abusing, yet how could a man turn his back on his own homeland? Wouldn't he feel enough love for it to want to work together with his fellow countrymen to make up for the evils they had committed, and to try to rebuild the nation? It grieved us to think that Mizushima wanted to live an easy life as a monk in another country, instead of returning to face the hardships awaiting us at home.

It was the old timer who shed the bitterest tears. He had believed that Mizushima died a splendid death, sacrificing himself to save his compatriots; and now Mizushima had turned out to be a deserter.

The old timer was a sincere man with a rigid sense of duty, the kind of man who would never dream of betraying anyone. From the time the captain became despondent, he took over the job of keeping our morale high. As a singer, though, he was undoubtedly the worst of "the singing company."

Before entering the army he had been a lower-grade office worker. I met him once after our discharge. He and his large family lived in a dilapidated house; he went back and forth to work day after day on crowded streetcars, wearing a faded old suit. He looked pale and undernourished, but didn't have a word of complaint.

I cannot help being appalled by what I read in newspapers and magazines nowadays. Many people seem to pride themselves on slandering and blaming others. "It's all that fellow's fault," they declare, as arrogantly as if we had won the war. "That's why the country is in such a mess." But these are the very people whose attitude during the war was hardly admirable, and who manage to live extravagantly even now. However, men like the old timer say nothing and simply keep on working. That seems to me far better than clamoring for your own selfish interests. No matter how chaotic things are, some people go on working silently and unobtrusively. Aren't they the real patriots? Doesn't the survival of a country depend on them?

Even on the morning of our departure we felt no profound emotion at leaving Burma behind us forever. Our thoughts were all of what lay ahead. We were going back to Japan. We didn't know what might have become of them in the meantime, but we were returning to our homes. Nor did we know what would become of us, but we were about to begin our lives over again.

We all sat around on our packs, talking about what we were going to do.

"When I get back I'll take a long nap on the veranda of my white-walled house among the mulberry trees. I'll hear the cool rippling of the stream, and now and then the plop of almonds on the roof above me. In the silkworm room the worms will be nibbling sleepily on mulberry leaves, and soon each of them will be spinning his white cocoon. I'll go back to that happy, busy life of taking care of them. . . ."

"Well, I'll be working in a factory. Over the roar of motors I'll hear a metallic whine and see shiny little nuts and bolts come tumbling out. That's my specialty."

"I'll be signaling trains at the railroad station. At night I used to be responsible for it all alone."

"I'm going to go whistling along on my bicycle, delivering vouchers around the Ginza. And on my way back to the office I'll stop in for a movie and a snack."

At that point the old woman arrived. Today she seemed quiet and gloomy, not her usual talkative self. She sat on the ground, spread her wares around her, and passed out longans and mangoes to all of us. Their pungent fragrance, full of the sunshine of the tropics, penetrated our eyes and noses. Knowing this was the last time we would be able to accept her generosity, we thought the fruit tasted better than ever.

The old woman pulled a bird out of the folds of her dress. It was the parakeet.

"Thanks for delivering our message," one of the soldiers told the bird. "But it didn't do much good, did it?"

The parakeet shook his gleaming green head, which shone as if it were jeweled, and peered about curiously for a moment. Then he shrieked out in Japanese, in a high singsong voice, "Ah, I cannot go home!"

"He's learned something new!" we exclaimed.

Just then the old timer came up. When he saw the parakeet he frowned. "That bird's no use to us any more. Let's get rid of him!" He grabbed the parakeet by the legs, and the bird stretched his neck, screeched, and beat his wings.

The old woman hurriedly retrieved him. Holding the parakeet against her breast, she said, "Look here, this is the big brother, the one the monk carried on his shoulder all along. See how much sleeker and nicer his plumage is! The monk's keeping the one you sent him, and asked me to bring you this one in exchange."

"Really?"

The parakeet cried again, "Ah, I cannot go home!"

"One more thing from that monk," the old woman went on, rummaging around in her dress again. She produced a thick envelope. "He asked me to deliver this to the captain. Since it was a monk that asked me, and it's the last favor I'll be doing you, I brought it."

We all gathered close to look at the letter. Its envelope appeared to be Burmese—long, rectangular, of good quality paper, the old-fashioned kind of envelope you'd expect a monk to use. As the old timer took it his big hands trembled. He stared grimly at it as if perplexed.

We called the captain, who had been busy settling our affairs. By now he had fully recovered and was as brisk and cheerful as ever. When he was handed the bulky envelope he hastily started to tear it open—but then stopped and said, "No, we're leaving shortly. Let's read it later, when we have more time."

"But, captain," the old timer objected, "can't you open it right now? Maybe there's a chance that Mizushima . . ."

"No." The captain shook his head calmly. "Mizushima isn't going back to Japan. It's no use reading this letter now."

The old timer sat down on the ground and heaved a long sigh. The captain put the letter into his breast pocket and buttoned the flap over it. "There's nothing to worry about," he said consolingly. "I'm sure this letter will please you."

When it was finally time to leave, Japanese soldiers streamed out of all the camps at once. Everyone waved to the old woman, who was standing by the gate. She craned her neck to watch after us as we marched away.

A few hours later we boarded a troopship at a small

river port. The pier was strewn with steel girders and lumber. We crossed a gangplank and climbed down a steep ladder into the narrow, crowded hold.

It was some time before our ship was ready to sail. The hot walls of the hold vibrated as steam hissed and engines started and stopped. On the deck overhead men shouted, hoists creaked, chains were wound and unwound, heavy crates dumped down—you could hear all the noisy confusion of loading cargo. As we sat together hugging our knees in that cramped, boxlike compartment, listening to what was going on around us, we felt a sudden sense of relief. Tears glistened in our eyes.

Through the portholes we saw a muddy, sluggish river lined with a rank growth of weeds and trees. An odor like rancid oil rose from the water. Boats with sails like huge outspread butterfly wings plied up and down. Now and then a small steamboat would proudly go puttering by between them, sending up a curling wreath of smoke.

We could see a harbor town of wooden shacks. People in *longyi* were walking around. Dogs were running along a road lined with palm trees. Fishermen were launching their boats. Everything looked so peaceful that it was hard to believe there had been a war in this country. Far in the distance stretched a zigzag chain of gray mountains.

That night, before we realized it, our ship had put out to sea.

CHAPTER TWO

BY THE third day we were used to our life aboard ship. When we went on deck that day we saw that we were passing through a wide channel, with the Malay Peninsula to the left and Sumatra to the right. We were spellbound by the beauty of the southern seas.

The sea, the sky, the islands all sparkled like brilliant gems. Clusters of emeralds and opals seemed to be floating side by side. A sky studded with white clouds was reflected in the mirror-like ocean; between them the great land masses wheeled slowly around us. All sorts of oddly shaped inlets and villages and lighthouses would emerge sharply into view, and then disappear behind another promontory. The sea breeze was pleasantly bracing. The constant lapping of the water against the ship made us feel as though our hearts were being washed clean. The sun was hot, the breeze cool, and we felt as if we were flying instead of sailing.

We went out on the stern deck and sat under a fluttering awning. The captain took the letter out of his breast pocket. "Well, let's have a look at it," he said. Carefully, almost reverently, he opened the envelope and took out a packet of about thirty sheets closely filled with minute handwriting.

The captain glanced around. "I guess you're all here," he said. "Now we'll read Mizushima's letter. The fact is, back in Mudon I got pretty depressed because he hadn't returned to us. And after I decided he might still be alive, so many weird things happened that I felt even more upset. I'm sorry I made you worry. Before long I came to believe that Mizushima must be that Burmese monk. But I hesitated to say anything until I had more evidence. In the meantime we found out that it *was* Mizushima, and we even got this letter.

"Still, why didn't he come back to us, and what was he doing disguised as a priest? I thought I knew the answer when I saw that box in the mortuary hall. The riddle was solved, as far as I was concerned. I know Mizushima. I think this letter will show that I wasn't mistaken about him." With that, the captain began to read:

My Dear Comrades:

I cannot tell you how much I long to see you, how much I would like to return to my company, to work with you, to talk and sing with you. I will never forget the joys and hardships we shared in this foreign land. Above all I cannot tell you how much I wish to return to my country, so fearfully changed, and to be reunited with my family.

Many times I secretly watched you as you went out on your construction jobs, or sang in the camp. Even when I was far away I would think longingly of you, and be drawn inevitably back to Mudon. Time and again I stood outside your fence till the first gray of dawn, looking at the thatch-roofed hut where you were sleeping. But now even that consolation is gone.

I shall not return to Japan. I have made a pledge to stay behind in Burma. Dressed as you saw me, I shall travel all over this country, into its mountains and along its rivers. There is a task to be done here. I cannot leave until I have finished it. Years from now, when my work is done, I may try to return to Japan. Or perhaps I may spend the rest of my life here, now that I am a monk, a servant of the Buddha. Whatever I do, I shall obey His will.

I have been taking care of the Japanese dead who lie scattered throughout this country. I dig graves for them and bury their whitened bones, to give them a final resting place. Hundreds of thousands of my young countrymen were drafted into the army, only to be defeated, routed, killed—and now their remains lie abandoned. It is a tragic sight. Once I saw it, I felt I had to care for these forgotten corpses. Until I have somehow accomplished that task, I cannot bring myself to leave.

As the captain said, I thought we should all return to Japan and work together to rebuild our nation. I still want to do that. But once I saw the dead that were being left behind, I knew I had to relinquish that desire. And this is not merely my own decision. Rather, a gentle but firm voice demands it of me. I can only bow my head and listen to this soft, irresistible voice.

After today's parting song, which I accompanied on my harp, I am at last fully reconciled to staying here. I shall remain behind. Please go home in good spirits—and work hard for me too.

Now I shall give you an account of all that happened to me since the day I left you in that mountain village.

* * *

When the captain had read that far, the old timer closed his eyes and clasped his hands in prayer. Some of the other men followed his example.

The parakeet was perched on the awning cord. Just then he cried out in a high, singsong voice, "Ah, I cannot go home!" The words trailed away in a mournful sigh.

We looked up. The green parakeet cocked his head to one side and looked down at us.

As the captain went on reading, his face beamed with pleasure. No doubt he had guessed right.

* * *

I hurried along the path with the British soldier and the guide, but it was nearly four o'clock in the afternoon when we reached the rocky mountain. After that, I seemed almost to be walking through a heavy fog—nothing is clear in my mind. I am not even sure of the sequence of events. My memories are only fragmentary, yet as vivid as if it all happened yesterday.

As we went on through the forest I heard the rumble of cannon fire becoming louder and louder. The forest was dense enough to screen out the sun, but still we could see an occasional lightning-like flash among the trees—and then, as we counted, " . . . three, four, five," we would be shaken by a thunderous explosion. The treetops shivered in its wake. All the birds had flown away; there was not a twitter. I did see a pair of giant lizards about two feet long. Their jaws were locked around each other, and they seemed to be dead.

Finally we came out of the forest into sudden full daylight. Straight ahead of us towered the gray triangular peak. It was a tremendous bald mass of rock—a sheer cliff rising from a winding river bed, its entire face honeycombed with holes. It looked as if it had been quarried for its stone, or used as a cliff dwelling. Apparently the holes were connected inside by a network of tunnels. Thin gun smoke drifted out of the mouths of these caves and crawled up the rock cliff, quietly rising in the brilliant sunshine. Now and then there would be a flash of rifle smoke. The whole dry, desolate peak seemed to be alive.

The headquarters of the attacking British troops was in the forest. Thanks to the soldier who came with me, I was able to see the commanding officer immediately. He was middle aged with gray hair, a man who looked as if he had good judgment. After listening to what I had to say, he gazed steadily at me for a moment and then made his decision.

"All right," he said. "See if you can get them to surrender. But I'll give you just thirty minutes—not a second longer." As I saluted and turned to leave, he called after me, "Good luck!"

I headed from the British camp toward the triangular peak, running through the trenches between them. This area seemed to have been a Japanese position at one time, but now it was a no man's land strewn with charred and splintered trees. The dead lay where they had fallen. There were smashed cannons; the ground was littered with handles, cogwheels, jagged scraps of metal of all kinds. Even the earth was scorched. It was a scene of incredible holocaust.

Just as I was climbing out of the last trench and over

a rocky outcrop, a burst of rifle fire from the peak spattered bullets around my feet. The bamboo grove behind me rustled as if in a gust of wind, and trees toppled over, felled by a great invisible scythe. I dropped flat. All this seemed curiously quiet, as I remember it. I only saw the bullets ricochet off the rock and the bamboo topple slowly. I shouted toward the peak, but even my own voice seemed to belong to someone else.

After a while I stood up and waved, but I was greeted with another burst of fire. Machine-gun bullets stitched a seam around me, and dust rose from each stitch. The rock chipped, and grass started to burn. I dropped flat again.

Since it was useless to keep on doing this, I jumped down from the outcrop and began running straight ahead. They must have recognized me as Japanese, for the firing stopped abruptly. I scrambled up the face of the rocky mountain. Some Japanese soldiers reached out of a cave and hauled me in.

"You made it!" They seemed delighted to see me.

"How'd you do it?"

"Where's your outfit?"

"You've got plenty of nerve!" Someone filled a mess tin lid to the brim with what seemed to be water, and gave it to me. "Here, drink this." I drank it down in one gulp. Then I realized that it was sake.

"We're going to fight it out," one of them told me. "You can join us—don't you have a gun? Well, take this one." He handed me a rifle.

A man who looked like their captain came in through a tunnel. It was so dark in the cave that at first I could hardly make out anything, but by now I saw a large group of men huddled together at the mouth of the tunnel, looking at me. "Glad to see you!" they said, with strained, contorted smiles. "How's your outfit doing?" All of them were stripped for action, naked from the waist up; their thin bodies were black with gun smoke, and their eyes were bloodshot.

The captain was a broad-shouldered man with a round, flushed face and a short mustache. He looked extremely tenacious. I could see at once that his men loved him. He was elated at this chance to show an outsider that his company was fighting to the death. As he gripped my hand, his eyes sparkled.

"We're really giving it to them, aren't we?" he said. "Pretty good morale, eh?" Then he asked if I had brought a message.

Standing at attention before him, I stated my mission. I told him what had happened to the other Japanese forces, and urged him to surrender.

Suddenly, while I was still trying to explain the situation, the captain roared, "That's enough!" The blood vessels on his forehead and neck stood out purple with rage; he was so furious he could hardly talk. "Surrender!" he blurted out violently. "How dare you say surrender! That's disgusting! If we surrendered now, we'd be insulting the men who have already died. Our company isn't cowardly like yours. We're going to fight till we're wiped out!"

"What good will it do to be wiped out?" I said. "We've got to live. We've got to live and struggle and work, for the sake of our country."

"For the sake of our country!" one of the soldiers exclaimed scornfully, glancing over at his captain. "What's so patriotic about surrendering?"

"We don't have any cowards like that in *our* company!" said another. He looked at the captain too. The captain nodded approvingly.

"If nobody at home surrenders how can Japan lose?"

They all talked that way, meanwhile gulping down sake which they dipped from an open keg in the middle of the cave.

As I listened I felt that these raging men were controlled by a strange force. Perhaps they were thinking different thoughts, but as a group their individuality had faded away. Having incited one another with a false show of courage, they could no longer back down. They could no longer take a different attitude. Something other than the will of the individual was making decisions and manipulating the group. I was at a loss as to how to come to grips with this stubborn thing. No doubt some of the men were determined to fight to the death—yet there also seemed to be those who doubted if that was the right course of action. But they could not speak out. Besides being too weak to resist the crowd, they were ignorant of the actual situation. They had no way to judge it. Even if they wanted to assert their opinion, they had nothing solid to build on. That is why the spirited but reckless argument had won the day—or so it seemed.

"Get out! You're no Japanese, a dirty coward like you. Go on, get out!"

"No, I'm staying till you come to your senses."

"If you don't go, you'll die here—you'd hate to lose your precious life, wouldn't you?"

"I don't want to throw my life away for nothing."

"Oh? You think we're fighting for nothing?"

"It's no use to your country or to yourselves. There's no point to it."

"Traitor!"

One of the soldiers tried to hit me. I dodged and his fist struck the harp I had slung over my shoulder.

"What's that thing?" he shouted. "Why are you fooling with a thing like that?"

"I use it to send secret messages!" I shouted back.

Time was running out. I spoke to the captain once more. "Sir, you're responsible for the lives of these men," I told him point blank. "If they die needlessly, can you accept the blame? Can you justify yourself to your country, and to their families?"

The captain caught his breath, as if he had been slapped in the face. He hesitated a moment, then turned and said, "All right. Just for the record, let's see what everybody thinks."

At his command, the men filed through a small opening at the back into another cave, leaving a guard behind with me.

I looked at my watch. Only ten minutes left.

I felt nervous and impatient. There were loud voices in the other cave. I yelled in, "Please make up your minds in the next five minutes!"

The guard whispered, "How do things stand, anyway?" He seemed very uneasy. Then he went on, as if muttering to himself, "There are lots of wounded men in that cave, and they all say they want to get it over with. . . . "

I could hear the captain asking questions and the men shouting back their answers. A few minutes later they returned, in a state of high excitement. Obviously the spirit that had carried them this far was still intact. If I could have talked with them quietly for an hour or so I might have been able to change some of their minds, but under this kind of pressure nothing could be done. There was exactly five minutes left.

Fixing his eyes on me, the captain delared in a loud voice, "Every man here is resolved to defend our position to the death. That's that."

I was speechless. I could feel the blood rush to my head. Some of the soldiers were crying, "Banzai!"

Dazedly, I started toward the mouth of the cave. All I could do now was ask the British commander to give me a little more time

As I reached the opening, insults were hurled at my back.

"Weakling! Coward! Go on and save your own skin!"

But their voices sounded pitiful. They were the bitter, envious voices of the doomed, flung at a man who would go on living.

I flew into a rage and shouted wildly, "I'm no coward!"

"Why are you giving yourself up then?"

"Is life so dear to you?"

Looking back, I saw them huddled miserably together with their arms around each other's shoulders.

"Listen!" I yelled. "In three minutes the British attack. I'll go out and be first to die. When I die, you surrender. You'll see if I'm a coward!"

I jumped down from the cave and dashed over to a tree stump in the no man's land between the cliff and the British position. Putting one foot up on the stump, I set the harp on my knee and started to play.

About a minute later the British opened fire. The Japanese on the peak returned it. Smoke and the acrid smell of gunpowder drifted into my nostrils. Soon it enveloped me like a thick fog, in the midst of which, feeling half numb, I plucked away at my harp.

Bullets whizzed past my ears with the shrill crack of a whip. I heard blood-curdling noises of splitting and rending all around me. The rocky face of the cliff began to chip away here and there. The British position was under heavy fire too.

At the beginning I could not hear the sound of my own harp. But after a while the music penetrated my deafened ears. Gradually it swelled louder, and as I listened I felt as if my body and soul were floating in a void. At last the harp was really singing. It had never sounded so loud and clear before. The air was thick with swirling, choking gun smoke.

"Sing!" I shouted as I lashed my harp. "Sing till your strings snap! When you're through singing and I'm dead, the men will be saved."

But then a bullet struck the harp with a thud, scattering the orchids and red feathers that decorated it. The harp was ruined.

"Now I'm done for!" I cried.

My mission was a total failure. . . . I stood there in blank dejection, the harp dangling from my hand. And then I felt something like the blow of a club against my thigh, a blow that knocked me over. I tried to jump to my feet but tumbled back again. My leg felt cold and wet, and I saw that it was bleeding.

As I lay on the ground I knew that I was slowly losing consciousness. Somehow I had a feeling of calm and relaxation. It was as if nothing more concerned me, I had no sense of dread or fear. I recall gazing dully at the scene as if I were watching lantern slides. A white flag dangled in the mouth of a cave. Then Japanese soldiers came pouring out. The British troops ceased fire.

Drowsily I looked up at the sky. I remember fluffy white clouds floating in an intensely blue evening sky. The sky and the surrounding mountains seemed to be rushing toward me at a furious speed.

Some time later I saw men carrying things out of the caves of the rocky mountain. My mind had begun to clear a little. I was so thirsty my throat seemed to be on fire. Then I became aware of the sound of running water somewhere below me. Without thinking, I started to crawl toward it. I could not yet feel the pain of my wound but my whole body was stiff, as if bound and fettered.

I kept on crawling until I reached a flat boulder near the foot of the mountain. I could hear a waterfall below. When I leaned forward, the boulder tipped over the edge of a low bluff. I fell, and everything went black.

CHAPTER THREE

WHEN I came to, I was lying in a primitive thatch-roofed hut cooled by a pleasant breeze. My wound had been carefully bandaged. I was on a soft leather mattress stuffed with feathers. The people nursing me were savages.

Even now there are many different tribes of savages in the mountains of Burma. Some of them are cannibals or head-hunters. It seems that while I was lying unconscious under the bluff the British troops rounded up their Japanese prisoners and withdrew, after which these savages happened to come by and rescue me.

The natives of this tribe were practically naked, their whole bodies decorated with tattoos and patterned scars. They wore iron rings around their ankles and wrists. Their eyes were turned up at the corners, their lips thick and jutting. But they were very courteous and gentle and seemed unlikely to harm me.

Indeed, as the days went by I realized just how kind and gentle they were. I was treated as a guest, given excellent care, and feasted every day. And such feasts! They kept urging all sorts of delicious, nourishing foods on me, and would get annoyed if I tried to refuse. Sometimes the situation became quite difficult. While I was recuperating in this village I lived a really extraordinary life.

My injury was from a rifle bullet in my thigh, and it healed faster than I had expected. At first I was terribly emaciated, but before long I began gaining weight, and I felt better every day.

The old man who brought my food was pleased to see how well I was recovering. Now and then he would circle his fingers around my arms and legs to measure them. I was putting on so much weight that in three days there would be a difference of almost one joint of the old man's fingers. Then he would screw up his wrinkled face in a toothless, happy grin and urge me to have some crocodile soup, or tropical fruits.

"Thank you, thank you," I would say, and eat my fill.

Since I had nothing else to do, I sat up in bed and made a new harp. Materials were limited, but I had bamboo of all sizes and I could use cowhide or sheep gut for the strings. I had had plenty of experience in making harps.

One day the village chief and his daughter came to see me. The chief was a towering giant with a stern, coal-black face, a man of majestic dignity. He studied my condition as closely as if he were a doctor examining a special case. Then he complained to the old man that I needed better care—I was still much too thin, and it was all because of his negligence. The old man apologized abjectly.

I hastened to intercede, saying, "Oh, no! He treats me very well. I owe my life to him."

The old man patted my body here and there, to show the chief how I had fattened.

The daughter attended to my wound. For a savage, she was an unusually shy, sweet girl. In applying herbs to the still unhealed wound, she sighed repeatedly and seemed genuinely sorry for me.

I played a tune for her on the harp. I was still so weak that playing made me gasp for breath. The chief's daughter was extremely sympathetic, and listened as if deeply moved; soon, her eyes still fixed on me, she began to shed tears. She looked as worried as if I were on the verge of death. "Do you think I'm going to die?" I said to her. "Just look at me!" I flexed my sleek, well-filled-out arms. Then I tried to stand up but there was still no strength in my legs, and I toppled back again on the feather bed.

The girl dabbed at her tears.

When the chief was ready to leave, I bowed to him and thanked him for his kindness. He smiled, baring his curved teeth, and nodded. "Please try this," he said, and gave me some of the choice betel nut which he was chewing. Though uncivilized, they are truly a good-natured and gentle people, I thought.

They took such good care of me that I soon recovered. About that time the moon was waxing, each night rising larger over the thatched rooftops, and as it brightened, a gayer and gayer spirit seemed to well up in the village.

There's a festival coming, I thought. One night, when the moon was nearly full and there was a great deal of noisy merriment going on outside, the old man brought me an especially fine dinner, which included a whole barbecued chicken. I had never eaten such delicious food, or so much of it, since the tide of war turned against us. I clasped the old man's hands in gratitude. He replied by stroking my nicely rounded body.

After that we talked for a while. To be sure, our conversation was a mixture of gestures and Burmese words, but by now we were quite expert in communicating with each other.

"I am glad you are so healthy," he said. "That makes me happy too." Outside in the moonlight natives were playing the flute joyfully.

"Thanks to you," I said, bowing.

"You ate what I brought you, so my job was easy. The other prisoners gave me much trouble by refusing to eat."

"I feel as strong as ever, and I intend to reward you for your kindness in some way."

The old man pinched my neck thoughtfully and said: "Now there must be enough for everybody."

"What?"

"Even if everybody in the village has a slice, there ought to be enough to go around."

"You mean you're going to eat me!"

"Yes, of course," the old man said, pursing his wrinkled mouth into a smile. "I am grateful to you for getting so nice and fat."

What a situation! I thought, looking down at my plump body, soft from lack of exercise. So this was a village of cannibals—and I had let them stuff me with all that food!

I asked the old man the name of his tribe, and he mentioned a certain name. I had heard of this tribe, who number about 250,000. They are head-hunters, and eat human flesh. When they take a man captive they put him down beside a bonfire to make him sweat, and then soak up his sweat in dumplings, which they eat. After that they cook him.

Though cannibals, they do not kill indiscriminately, but only when they consider it necessary for purposes of magic. They live in constant terror of invisible evil spirits, which they believe to be all around them. These fierce-looking savages are actually timid. When they pray for a rich harvest, they try to appease the spirits by offering them something very precious—a human head. They eat the victim's flesh because they hope to add his strength to their own, and thus become a better match for the evil spirits. As a result, these people are dangerous only around the time of the harvest festival. When that is over, they are mild and well behaved.

Everywhere in Burma people believe in spirits called *nats*. The spirits live in trees, rocks, and other natural objects, and if they love you, good fortune will come your way. But if you anger them you will suffer a dreadful calamity. All Burmese—even intellectuals—worship the *nats*. I have often seen people making offerings to them, or performing ceremonies to propitiate them. These savages too worshiped the *nats*, and had erected many small shrines to them.

"When am I to be eaten?" I asked the old man.

"The festival is tomorrow!"

By this time there was no use refraining from food, so I finished off the barbecued chicken. But somehow my mouth felt dry; the chicken seemed unappetizing. The old man kept gazing at my body fondly.

I was surprisingly calm. After all, I was dealing with simple, primitive people. Something will work out, I thought, making light of my predicament. It would have been difficult to escape then anyhow, and it might even have been to my disadvantage. I was relying on my harp.

In a pinch, I can use the harp, I told myself. As long as I have that . . . I slept well that night, hugging my harp close to me.

The next morning at sunrise I was stripped naked, taken out to a boulder in the river, and scrubbed from head to toe, so vigorously it hurt. The natives cleansed themselves too. Then I was put inside a decorated cage, where I sat holding my harp. They carried the cage to the center of the village and placed it on the ground before a shrine.

The shrine was a small thatch-roofed building enclosed by a bamboo fence. There was an altar in front of it displaying the sacrificial offerings of a bull's head and entrails. Tall poles with crossbars at the top stood all around. They seemed to have some magical significance. Beside the shrine was a huge tree with thick foliage. Every part of it, from its roots to its branches, was sacred to the *nat* spirits.

Finally the ceremonies began. The men of the tribe performed various sacrificial rites, chanted incantations, and then took up their knives and spears and started dancing.

They wore large bonnet-like feathered headpieces, their ears hidden by round bone ornaments as big as the palm of a hand. Forming a long line, they began shouting in rhythm, crouching, stamping their feet, shaking their hips, gradually working themselves into a frenzy. Now and then they turned toward the *nat*-tree, and seemed to be praying, or pressed their heads to the ground and shuddered, violently. At last they started going round and round my cage, singing and occasionally shrieking as if in terror. Their knives and spears were flashing back and forth rhythmically just before my eyes. They seemed about ready to drag me out and kill me.

Now is the time, I thought, coolly taking up the harp and starting to play. I felt confident. As long as I have my harp I can win them over, I thought. Sitting cross-legged inside the cage chewing betel nut and grinning broadly, I played all the best songs I knew, both gay and sad.

It was no use. The savages were not soothed by my music. No matter how hard I played, or how moving the song, they did not respond as I had hoped. On the contrary, they waved their knives and spears more vigorously than ever, keeping time with my harp, and danced and prayed to the *nats* in wild delirium. It was a disgusting spectacle.

Before long they piled up an enormous heap of firewood, lighted it, dragged me out of the cage and bound my legs, and put me down beside the bonfire. All the while I kept playing my harp, trying to make them change their minds. But it was useless.

The heat was so fierce I could hardly stand it. I began to sweat more and more profusely. I felt as if my whole body were immersed in hot water. Even my hair was soaked.

The savages gathered in a ring around me, each with a dumpling in his hand. After rubbing the dumplings against my skin and saturating them with perspiration, they raised them reverently to their heads and ate them. Not far away some of the others were already sharpening knives.

I was desperate. The sweat ran. The heat was intense. Soon they would make a meal of me—how I regretted having taken my danger so lightly!

Then a wind sprang up. The flames of the bonfire fanned out over me, almost burning me alive. The savages kept giving me water, and I kept on sweating. The wind became stronger and stronger. As it roared through the trees, charred leaves came fluttering down on my naked body.

I felt giddy, and so thirsty I cried out for more water. Now, though, they refused to bring me any. Also, they stopped wiping my body with dumplings. So this is the end, I thought, and closed my eyes.

After a little while I opened my eyes again and was surprised to see everyone standing around looking anxious. They were staring at the great *nat*-tree, which was swaying and groaning in the wind.

Another gust of wind shook the tree. The savages covered their ears and prostrated themselves on the ground. Some clasped their hands and prayed. Some raised their arms whenever the tree groaned, as if to ward off an unseen attack. Because the tree was raging, they were afraid they had angered the spirits.

This is my chance! I thought. Lying there on my back with my feet bound, still clutching my harp, I started playing the ceremonial music that the Burmese use in worshiping the *nats*. As I played, I shouted, "*Nat!*" When the wind roared again, I struck frightening sounds from the strings. The savages screamed in terror.

I kept on shouting, "*Nat!*" and shrieking nonsense. Then I made runs that sounded like evil spirits swooping down, hovering and laughing, or angrily attacking. The great tree rocked from side to side. Men howled and trembled with fear. I played as hard as I could, following the movements of the tree.

Gradually the savages withdrew, hiding their faces, but

at last they came crawling timidly up to me and untied my bonds. I staggered to my feet, trying to look as haughty as possible, and went over to sit next to the chief.

The wind was still blowing, so I played something quiet to calm the spirit of the *nat*-tree. Finally, the savages relaxed.

After that a lively party began under the bright full moon. The wind slacked off to a cool, refreshing breeze, and dew glistened on the millet.

The chief drank copiously from a water-buffalo horn, and urged me to drink too. According to tribal custom, it would have been a mortal insult to refuse. There were spears and knives and guns all around. Since I could not afford to anger them I accepted their liquor and tried to drink cautiously. But in the end I got thoroughly drunk. Everything was blurred, and danced merrily before my eyes.

The chief was in high spirits, singing and eating lustily. But suddenly he drained the horn to the bottom, set it down, and leaned his ferocious face close to mine.

"You—" he growled, baring his teeth, "You marry my daughter." He narrowed his bloodshot eyes and added, "Or I'll cut your head off."

* * *

When the captain read these lines, we couldn't help laughing.

"What a problem for a serious-minded fellow like Mizushima!"

"In his situation, I'd gladly marry a cannibal's daughter!"

The captain laughed too and went on reading.

* * *

I was stunned. I could see the girl sitting there shyly with downcast eyes.

Looking very grave, the chief stood up and gave one

hand to his daughter and one to me. He faced the crowd of tribesmen and began a solemn speech. He spoke as if we were already engaged.

"My people, I wish to apologize for the poor fare tonight, and for all the faults in the ceremony. . . . Now this bridegroom is a fine young man, and if I could give each of you a piece of his flesh tonight it would have a marvelous effect on our fighting strength. However, as you all saw, this young man has the power to talk to the *nats*. If we kill him, what will the spirits do? And so, as your chief, I have chosen what is best for the village. Instead of eating him, I want to marry him to my daughter, and add his strength to ours in that way. . . ."

The crowd applauded enthusiastically.

I felt bewildered—by now I was cold sober. But there was nothing I could do. Like any bridegroom, I stood looking down meekly as if resigned to my fate.

But the chief had paused only to whisper to me, "How many heads have you taken so far?"

I whispered back, "None."

The chief frowned, and whispered angrily, "This is no time for jokes. Ten? Twenty? If it's not enough, I lose face in front of my people. You can exaggerate a little. Now hurry up, how many?"

Good! I thought, I won't have to marry his daughter after all. Then I answered in a deliberately loud voice, so that everyone could hear, "Never in all my life have I taken a human head."

The chief exploded. He tore his hair and stamped the ground, shouting, "Never? Not even one? I can't give my daughter to a spineless coward! I think we *will* eat you!"

But his daughter threw her arms around him and pleaded for my life.

That was how the festival ended. Afterward the tribe released me.

When I left, the whole village came to see me off. The

chief's daughter regretted my leaving most of all. She outfitted me in the robes of a Burmese monk, telling me I would have no trouble wherever I went. And she also gave me an armband of tin engraved with a verse from the sutras. I thought it was only a souvenir, but actually it was the badge of a monk of high rank. Thanks to it, I was able to enjoy all sorts of later advantages.

To Mudon! a voice cried within me, as I started briskly off. Coming to the steep flight of stone steps outside the village, I turned to look back and saw the slight figure of the chief's daughter. She was praying at the *nat* shrine.

CHAPTER FOUR

I HAD NO real idea how to get to Mudon—I simply kept traveling south, over mountains and through valleys. Presently I came to a plain dotted with Burmese villages.

I seemed to be walking on and on forever through a peaceful, languid garden of rice paddies. This was no longer the territory of savages, but of an ancient and high civilization. Here and there farmers were plowing their fields, using water buffaloes. As a buffalo started to move, snowy herons would fly down and perch on its back and horns. But they flew away again in fright whenever the buffalo reached the edge of the field and the farmer turned his plow.

Once, as I was walking along, a moist wind began to blow and the sky quickly filled with black clouds. Herons were tossing in the wind like downy feathers. Soon the rain came. Rainfall in Burma is violent. Before I knew it, I was shut in by a thick spray. I could hardly breathe—I felt as if I were swimming.

After a while the rain stopped and the sky cleared. All at once the landscape brightened and a vast rainbow hung across the sky. The mist was gone, as if a curtain had been lifted. And there, under the rainbow, the farmers were singing and plowing again.

In these villages people would kindly offer me alms whenever I stopped to pray at their door. Sometimes I stayed at a temple. But at the temples I was given such a warm welcome because of my armband that it made me uncomfortable, since I knew nothing about clerical customs and etiquette.

However, this country has Buddhist monks of all kinds. There are those who do penance by never saying a word as long as they live, or by hanging from trees for years, or deliberately acting insane—anything, no matter how strange, to mortify their flesh. They will face any hardship to achieve salvation. Some even crawl half naked across the snow-covered Himalayas. It is amazing how earnestly the people of this southern land have struggled to free themselves from bondage to their earthly existence and to attain enlightenment. For the most part I got along by keeping silent, as if practicing religious austerities. Then, too, the Burmese do not pry into the affairs of strangers, and so a man disguised as a monk can go anywhere unsuspected.

Still, I did have a few bad moments.

Once I entered a certain village that was ringing with the sound of gongs, drums, and harps. As soon as it was dusk the impatient villagers changed into their best *longyi,* put flowers in their hair, and streamed out of their houses.

That night a kind of dance-drama called the *pwè* was to be given. On such occasions a large group of gorgeously costumed young girls dance till dawn, bending and twisting supplely in time to the music. During the intervals between dances, plays are performed. The *pwè* has been in existence for centuries and is a favorite entertainment among the entertainment-loving Burmese.

"Monk, please come to our *pwè,*" one of the villagers said to me.

I refused brusquely. "In penance . . . no amusement . . ."

Soon another man came up to me and said, "Monk, there's a funeral too. Please come."

This time I could hardly refuse. I was led to a clearing at the outskirts of the village, and found a *pwè* already going on. Music and laughter rang out gaily. Young girls were singing and dancing in the twilight, repeating the same gestures over and over.

I took the seat that was assigned to me. It seemed odd to hold a funeral in such gay, noisy surroundings, but I could not inquire about it. Other Burmese monks were sitting there too. I was behind them and imitated everything they did.

The *pwè* became more and more lively, and the audience was enjoying it to the full. Soon a richly bedecked float appeared, drawn up near the dancers by a host of smiling men. The float carried a high, tower-like structure decorated from top to bottom with papier-mâché dolls and elephants, and ornamental scent-bags.

Then the cart was set afire, and the flaming bits of colored paper fluttered away toward the clouds glowing in the sunset. Everyone applauded happily at the sight.

Under the burning tower, a play began. A winged spirit appeared, drew a princess out of a lotus flower, taught magic to the prince who was searching for her, and the like. It reminded me of a children's pantomime.

I was wondering when the funeral would start. Still if I said anything I might expose my true identity, so I merely went on imitating the monks in front of me, keeping my hands clasped in prayer and mumbling under my breath.

Later, when the whole tower had burned down, people scooped the ashes away from the center of the float and threw in all sorts of beautiful ornaments. After that, a man handed each of us monks something like a pair of long chopsticks.

"Please come!" he said, leading us forward. I followed the other monks.

Where the ashes had been scooped away I could see the charred remnants of a kind of large box, within which, buried under gold and silver ornaments and fragrant flowers, lay the bones of a now cremated human body. The gay, festive float was actually a funeral pyre. After some urging, I helped take the bones out with my tongs.

Not far away, the *pwè* was going on at a lively pace. All the dancing girls lifted their arms and swayed their bodies, singing over and over again the gay, monotonous tune of a dramatic ballad. Music from stringed, wind, and percussion instruments mingled in the evening air and drifted endlessly through the village. The dance and the funeral seemed equally pleasurable.

I learned later that the Burmese do not fear death. Human beings must necessarily die, and death is the means of escaping earthly passions and returning to the source of life. When a man is dying here in Burma, people gather around and tell him of all his past good deeds, confident that the Buddha will lead him to a better world. And so a funeral is actually a happy farewell party.

As I was lifting out the bones, someone noticed my armband. Since a monk of such high rank is rarely seen in a country village, I was escorted to the place of honor—and asked to chant the sutras.

Another predicament! However, I managed to bluff it through with a trick that had worked once before in a similar situation. Suddenly I intertwined my legs in a meditative posture, drew one long breath, and then sat motionless, scarcely breathing, as if in deep contemplation.

For some time I remained in that posture, seemingly deaf, dumb, and blind. The villagers must have thought the holy monk had had some kind of revelation and was engaged in profound thought, his spirit off in a distant world. They left me to myself.

No matter where you go, the Burmese seem happy. They live and die smiling. All the troubles of this world and the next are left to the Buddha, as they pass their days tilling the soil, singing, and dancing, without selfishness or greed.

Burma is a peaceful country. Though weak and poor, it has flowers, music, resignation, sunshine, Buddhist images, smiles. . . .

CHAPTER FIVE

My only concern was to head south, as fast as I could, toward Mudon.

Before long I came to another mountainous region. After crossing several passes I found myself walking through desolate hills, where there were only dead trees and boulders piled upon boulders. I did not meet a single human being along the way.

As I was climbing a sandy road I happened to notice a rifle bullet at my feet. I picked it up and saw that it was a familiar Japanese type. Other bullets and cartridges lay all around.

How could they have got here? I wondered, and kept on climbing. Looking up, I saw a flock of birds circling low, round and round, just over a crag ahead of me. And then some black birds with large beaks and broad wings flew up from behind the crag. The sun was shining dully; there was not a sound to be heard.

Finally I reached the top of the pass—a barren gorge

without a blade of grass or a single tree. When I got there, I stood paralyzed with horror.

In the shadow of the red rock of the gorge lay the scattered remains of about thirty men and half a dozen horses. The bodies were completely dried up, with their white bones sticking out. Strewn among them were machine guns, rifles, leather knapsacks. A steel helmet lay where it had rolled to a stop. Everything was leveled flat, half buried in the reddish sand. Where the dead bodies were lying the grass grew luxuriantly. As I approached, a bird squawked and flew up past me, almost into my face.

This had been a party of Japanese soldiers, probably wiped out by an ambush or a bombing raid. Unknown to any of their comrades, they lay here abandoned. I gathered dry wood, built a fire, and started to cremate the corpses. But the job could not be finished in a day. Much as I was anxious to hurry on, I stayed overnight at the nearest village and went back the next day, and the day after, to burn more of the bodies. It took me about a week. Then I buried their ashes, set up a small grave marker over them, and joined my hands in prayer. All alone, I held a funeral service for these unfortunate men.

After that, I headed south once more. I shall refrain from going into detail about what I saw. It was unbelievably horrible. As a Japanese, as a fellow countryman of the dead, I was sorrowful beyond tears.

Once I was passing through a small woodland. It began to rain so hard that the road turned to mud, but I happened on a broken-down hut and went inside to rest.

There was a corpse in the hut—a corpse wearing a Japanese army uniform. Probably a sick or wounded soldier had dropped behind during a rout and then crawled into this hut and died. The body was black with swarming ants and maggots, but it was not too decomposed. Apparently the man had stayed alive in the hut for a fairly long time. Nearby lay a photograph of a young father holding a little boy. No doubt it was this dead man and his child.

It was impossible to burn the corpse in that leaking hut, so I carried it on my back into the woods and buried it there. I wondered what to do with the picture, but at last I buried it along with the dead man. It seemed to me he would have wanted it that way. I suppose the little boy has the same picture on his wall, somewhere in Japan, and often looks at it as he waits for his father to come home.

I found other corpses here and there in these woods, obviously left behind by fleeing troops. In southern Burma there is a place the Japanese called "Skeleton Road." That is where I have been recently—true to its name, it is even more horrible than the little woods.

And so I buried the bodies of Japanese soldiers wherever I found them. But I soon realized what an enormous task this was. Even those in the little woods took a long time to bury. Yet I could not abandon them. Nor was this the only place—I had no idea how many of my compatriots were lying unburied throughout the length and breadth of Burma. Truly the wailing voices of the dead were calling me. I've got to do *something,* I thought desperately. But I wanted to hurry to Mudon. I had to go there. I wanted to find out how my comrades were, I wanted to see them. I thought how happy I would be to return at last to my unit, how happy everyone would be to have me back. The longer I thought, the worse my dilemma seemed. Mudon was still far away, and at this rate it might take years to get there.

Anyway, I finally buried all the corpses I found in the woods, resumed my journey, and came to a wide river. It was the Sittang, swollen with swift-moving muddy water. While I was looking for a boat to ferry me across, I saw an appalling sight.

It was a mound of decomposing bodies. They had been dumped together into a swamp along the river, piled up in tepid water among thick rushes and frothy scum. They seemed to have been stripped of their belongings, clothes and all. Probably this was a crossing point for our troops, where many died in the retreat.

I covered my face. This task was beyond my strength. I could not begin to tackle it alone.

And so I gave up. I would not attempt to bury them. The dead are dead, I told myself; I won't give them another thought. I feel sorry for these unfortunate men, but they're no responsibility of mine—I can't stop to worry about every one of them. I'm going to rejoin my company, go back to Japan, and start a new life! That was what I wanted to do, from the bottom of my heart.

I had made my mind up and felt much relieved. I took a boat down the river, occasionally traveled overland by oxcart and train, and soon reached Mudon.

During my journey I had learned to speak Burmese rather fluently, as well as to conduct myself like a monk.

As I approached Mudon, my heart began to throb with excitement. I met a man in the woods at its outskirts and asked him about the town. He had just chopped down a tree to catch five parakeets and he gave me the greenest one. After that I took the bird with me wherever I went. And that is the bird I shall send along with this letter.

According to the man I talked to, there were Japanese P.O.W. camps in Mudon, and at one of them the prisoners were always singing. Then I knew you were still there, and I almost danced for joy as I hurried on into town. After making various inquiries, I found the camp. But by that time it was late at night, the camp was closed, and all I could see was a ray of lamplight from the window.

That night I stood by the fence with a full heart and stared at the camp until the light went out. Once I shivered when I heard a voice that sounded like the captain's. At last I gave up my post and went to ask for a night's lodging at a monastery in town.

The next morning I woke up while it was still dark. Eager to get to camp as fast as I could, I jumped out of bed and started to dress. Today I can join my company! I thought. It's been three months since I left them—a lot has happened in that time. I was so excited and happy that my hands trembled as I dressed. I put on a new yellow robe that had been given me at the monastery and picked up my begging bowl.

"They'll certainly be surprised to find me looking like this," I said to myself, laughing. "I know they'll be glad to see me."

It occurred to me that I had been awakened by the sound of a harp in the monastery garden. Someone was slowly picking out the melody of *Hanyu no Yado*. I listened for a while, until I could no longer resist the impulse to go and see who it was. There in the faint purple light of dawn a young Burmese boy sat practicing the harp. I went over to him and asked why he was playing so early in the morning.

"I'm sorry to have disturbed you, sir," he answered, bowing politely, "I sleep in the kitchen here, but every day I go out to earn money with my harp."

"Why do you play that tune?"

"Because the Englishmen pay to hear it."

There was still some time before the gate of the monastery would be opened. I took up the harp and softly played my own arrangement of the song. The boy listened wide eyed and then begged me to teach it to him. He said he would earn more if he played it that way.

I was feeling happy and joyful, and it pleased me to

think I could help him. Of course it was a good deal later before he mastered the whole of it.

That morning the boy told me an unexpected piece of news.

"There's a hospital in this town run by the English," he was saying. "When a patient dies they bury him in the hospital cemetery. The English doctors and nurses attend the funeral, and if I wait by the roadside and play this tune on their way back they even give me silver. According to the caretaker, there's going to be another funeral today. It seems a lot of Japanese soldiers held out in a cave in the mountains for a long time, but they finally surrendered and the wounded were brought to this hospital. People are talking about it all over town, saying how awful they looked. Some of them have died and they'll be buried together this morning. So if I go and play this song I'm sure to make money."

Are the wounded from that triangular peak? I wondered. What had happened to those men after I left? Even if I could not talk to them directly, I wanted to find out more about them. But that would be impossible once I entered camp, so I decided to go first to the hospital and investigate.

As soon as the monastery gate was opened I went with the boy to the hospital. But it was still so early in the morning that I could find no one to ask. No one was going in or out of the building.

Just then I heard voices singing a hymn. It was a mixed chorus, mostly women, and it was coming from the cemetery, which was in a little grove behind the hospital.

I went into the grove. The trees were wet with morning dew, and a fleecy white mist was still hanging in their branches. The tidy gravel paths reminded me of a park, and here and there wreaths of fresh or withered flowers lay before the neatly aligned crosses and coffin-shaped tombstones. In one of the far corners of the cemetery stood a group of English people.

Hiding behind a large eucalyptus tree, I watched them. Most of them were blue-eyed, rosy-cheeked nurses in fresh, trim uniforms. The men were bareheaded. The burial had just ended, and they were all singing a hymn beside the grave. After finishing their hymn, they crossed themselves, bowed their heads for a moment in prayer, and quietly walked away.

When they were gone I went up and found a new granite tombstone decorated with a small but pretty wreath. The stone bore the inscription: "Here Lie Unknown Japanese Soldiers."

I stood there for some time, bewildered. Then I heard the harp playing *Hanyu no Yado* near the gate of the cemetery. As if drawn by it, I started unsteadily toward the gate. I was burning with shame. How wretched I felt for having turned my back on those dead bodies heaped beside the river!

I could hear a fierce voice whispering deep within me: Foreigners have done this for us—treated our sick and wounded, buried our dead, prayed to console their spirits. You cannot leave the bones of your comrades to weather by the Sittang River, and in mountains, forests, and valleys that you have yet to see! *Hanyu no Yado* is not only a song of yearning for your own home, for your own friends. That harp expresses the longing of every man for the peace of his home. How would they feel to hear it, the dead whose corpses are left exposed in a foreign land? Can you go away from this country without finding some kind of resting place for them? Can you leave Burma? Go back! Retrace your steps! Think over what you have seen on your way here. Or do you just want to leave? Do you lack the courage to go back north?

I could not ignore that voice. An unexpected duty

had been thrust upon me, and I had to set about fulfilling it as soon as possible. Instead of going toward the camp, I headed straight out of town.

Still, I wanted to see my old comrades again, if only from a distance. My pace slackened. After turning back more than once, I finally went to the camp, but no one was there. I waited for hours—all of you were away on a construction job. Disappointed but unable to wait any longer, I set out once again as if I were being driven.

I hurried through the outskirts of Mudon, and was just crossing a narrow bridge, which seemed to have been newly repaired, when I saw you coming toward me. I did not recognize any of you, in your strange-looking, muddy P.O.W. clothes, until I was already halfway across the bridge. Then, as we came nearer, I found myself trembling with joy, sadness, embarrassment. I cannot describe to you all that was in my heart as we passed, making way for each other on that narrow bridge. At long last I had come face to face with my old friends and comrades, but by this time I was determined to go north. Since I could not rejoin you I had to keep myself from letting you know who I was. I had to let you think that Mizushima was dead.

After that, with the green parakeet on my shoulder, I walked ahead rapidly to the north.

CHAPTER SIX

WHEN THE captain had read this far, the parakeet on the awning cord cried out, "Ah, I cannot go home!" It's voice trailed off again in a mournful sigh. We all sighed too, and gazed out toward the ocean.

It was evening, and the vivid colors of the straits had faded. Now it was like a scene on a photographic neg-tive. Sumatra and the Malay Peninsula still wheeled slowly around us over the placid water. The inlets here and there were already deep in shadow, some of them twinkling with the lights of fishing boats at their moorings. The waves lapping monotonously against our hull made a lonely sound. Our ship had been gliding along smoothly, but as darkness fell it began to roll a little.

The captain went on reading.

* * *

I am now at a monastery, where I have spent the night writing this letter. It is almost dawn; the moon is low, hanging like a glowing lamp beneath the palm tree in the garden. There are many falling stars.

You can imagine how much I wanted to let you know that I was Mizushima. But If I were discovered to be a Japanese, I would have had to enter a P.O.W. camp. I would have had to abandon my new duty. I have begun many letters to you but then stopped, telling myself to forget past ties. Since I could not go home and work with you, it would have been painful for me to have you know that I was alive. And later, after I became a real Burmese monk, the man known as Corporal Mizushima no longer existed.

But even while burying my dead countrymen far away, I could not help thinking about you and getting restless. Then I would come back to Mudon and stand on the other side of the fence and listen to you sing. I would be overcome with nostalgia, remembering how I used to sing with you myself. I was always wondering anxiously when you would go home to Japan. And so I breathed a sigh of relief whenever I returned to Mudon and found my company still here.

My pet parakeet eventually picked up the words I used to murmur to myself. I suppose he is there at your side. In his place, your parakeet is perched on my shoulder. Now and then he calls out, "Hey, Mizushima! Let's go back to Japan together!" Somehow it always startles me.

However, I shall not go back—not until I have fulfilled my mission. Yesterday I lost control of myself, forgot my long-standing vow, and played the harp in farewell to you; and as I walked away from the camp the two parakeets on my shoulders screamed their appeals to me one after the other. I had to choose between them. But actually my choice was clear. The bones of the countless unknown dead are calling me. They are waiting for me. I cannot ignore them.

I am sure you will forgive me.

When I left Mudon for the first time I went straight to that Sittang River crossing point. During the rout of the Japanese army all communications were cut off and our troops fled in utter confusion, with the result that tragic losses of this kind occurred throughout Burma.

According to the natives who lived along this stretch of the Sittang, many Japanese units attempted a night crossing here. It was over two hundred yards across the swollen river, and they tried to make it with nine or ten men on each small raft. But the rafts would only get to midstream and then be swept down the river. Some must have been carried all the way out to sea, and others washed ashore in the heart of the jungle. They tried various other crossing points too, and at night the natives often heard cries for help from a raft drifting somewhere in the river.

Every crossing point took its toll of lives, but there were also many soldiers—especially those suffering from dysentery or malaria, or too weak from lack of food to keep going—who seized the first chance to kill themselves with a hand grenade. Explosions were often heard in the fields or woods after fleeing troops had passed through. Even the natives knew that each explosion meant another suicide.

There must have been a vast number of such incidents untold, unrecorded, merely forgotten!

How could anyone see what I have seen and do nothing about it? How could anyone ignore it with a clear conscience, or say that it was none of his business?

With the help of the natives and of the monks from a nearby village, I managed to bury these corpses in the sandy river bank. And while digging in the sand one day I found a large ruby—one of the famous Burmese rubies. It shone like a deep red flame of dazzling brilliance.

As I held it in my hand this jewel reminded me of the souls of the dead. Since I could not carry their ashes around with me, I regarded this ruby as symbolizing the spirits of all the men who had died here in Burma; and thereafter I always kept it on my person. Whenever I visited a temple I placed it on the altar to worship.

I heard that the English were to have a magnificent funeral service in Mudon, and I wanted this ruby to be part of it. Though it was wrong to start a war, how could the young men who had to fight and die be considered guilty? Whether English or Japanese, their souls had departed from this earth. To hope for a joint funeral, or at least for an inconspicuous place at this one, would surely not be resented by the English dead. On the contrary, they would probably smile and welcome the souls of the Japanese to their own altar. After all, in that mountain village on the night of the armistice living enemies took each other's hands. . . .

And so I put the ruby in a plain wooden box, wrapped the box in a cloth and hung it from my neck, and joined the funeral procession. Then I placed it in a corner of the altar in the mortuary hall.

During the several days of the memorial service this ruby too was paid homage with heartfelt gratitude. As the only Japanese present, I prayed constantly.

However, the ruby could not be left in the mortuary

hall forever. I had to find another place for it before the English dead were sent back to their homeland. I began searching for a secret place where it would be undisturbed—and hit on the idea of putting it in that huge reclining Buddha. After that I went inside the figure every day through an entrance in the sole of the Buddha's foot—an entrance known only to the monks of the nearby temple—to construct an altar and bury the box with the ruby.

One day, there in the dark, stifling hollow of the Buddha, I was feeling so tired I leaned against the wall to rest. As I was dozing off to sleep I heard you singing.

Startled out of my nap, I automatically snatched up my harp. Ever since beginning my journeys inland I had always taken my harp along with me. When I came to Mudon I often played with the boy at the monastery. So of course I had the harp with me that day too.

You must have been astonished to hear music coming from such an unlikely place. Please forgive me. But as I played my only thought was, Here I am! I'm alive! My dear comrades, let's sing together!

Afterward, when you were pounding on the door, I was standing just inside, fists clenched in anguish. I recognized every voice. But since I am now a monk, I could not throw open the door and embrace you.

Then it became very quiet, and I climbed a ladder to peep out through one of the Buddha's eyes. I saw you being led away toward the temple by an Indian soldier.

I have become a Burmese monk. After finishing those burials by the Sittang River, I went to a temple not far away and was permitted to take holy orders. I have continued to study whenever possible, and to practice religious austerities. I gave up the temple armband I had received from the chief's daughter; but later, in recognition of my efforts to bury the dead, I was given another armband.

The work I must do seems to grow day by day. Not only must I give solace to the spirits of the Japanese soldiers, but I must fulfill my duties as a Burmese monk. And I want to do all I can for the people of this country.

I want to study Buddhist teachings, to reflect on them and make them a part of me. We and our fellow countrymen have suffered cruelly. Many innocent people were sacrificed to a senseless cause. Fresh, clean young men were taken from their homes, jobs, and schools, only to leave their bones bleaching on the soil of a distant land. The more I think of it, the bitterer my sorrow. As I look back on what has happened, I feel keenly that we have been too unthinking. We have forgotten to meditate deeply on the meaning of life.

I have learned a great deal during my training as a monk. Since ancient times this religion has been dedicated to an extraordinarily profound meditation on human life and on the world in which it exists. Those who devote themselves to its teachings willingly undergo all sorts of dangerous trials and harsh austerities in order to grasp the truth. Their courage is as great as any soldier's; theirs is a battle to capture an invisible fortress. In this cause, as I have told you, some even crawl half naked up the snow-covered Himalayas.

We Japanese have not cared to make strenuous spiritual efforts. We have not even recognized their value. What we stressed was merely a man's abilities, the things he could do—not what kind of a man he was, how he lived, or the depth of his understanding. Of perfection as a human being, of humility, stoicism, holiness, the capacity to gain salvation and to help others toward it—of all these virtues we were left ignorant.

I hope to spend the rest of my life seeking them as a monk in this foreign land.

As I climbed mountains and forded rivers, and buried the bodies I found lying smothered in weeds or soaked in water, I was harassed by tormenting questions. Why does so much misery exist in the world? Why is there so much inexplicable suffering? What are we to think?

But I have learned that these questions can never be solved by human thought. We must work to bring what little relief we can to this pain-ridden world. We must be brave. No matter what suffering, what unreasonableness, what absurdity we face, we must remain undaunted and show strength of character by meeting it with tranquillity. It is my hope to realize this conviction by devoting myself to a religious life.

Furthermore, I never cease to marvel that the people of Burma, though certainly indolent, pleasure-seeking, and careless, are all cheerful, modest, and happy. They are always smiling. Free from greed, they are at peace with themselves. While living among them, I have come to believe that these are precious human qualities.

Our country has waged a war, lost it, and is now suffering. That is because we were greedy, because we were so arrogant that we forgot human values, because we had only a superficial ideal of civilization. Of course we cannot be as languid as the people of this country, and dream our lives away as they often do. But can we not remain energetic and yet be less avaricious? Is that not essential—for the Japanese and for all humanity?

How can we truly be saved? And how can we help to save others? I want to think this through carefully. I want to learn. That is why I want to live in this country, to work and serve in it.

My dear comrades, I cannot tell you what this parting means to me. The day I have long dreaded has at last arrived. When I came back to Mudon after many weeks in the interior I heard that my company was to sail for Japan the next morning. I was able to receive the news with unexpected calm.

I am very happy and grateful for your affection, for your reluctance to leave me behind. But I shall stay here in Burma, this country I love, and wander everywhere from its snow-capped mountains to its beaches under the glittering Southern Cross. And when my longing for you becomes too much to bear, I shall play my harp.

I shall never forget our friendship. I pray for your happiness from the bottom of my heart.

Mizushima Yasuhiko

CHAPTER SEVEN

THE CAPTAIN had finished the letter.

We all sat there in silence, filled with thoughts we could not express. But we were no longer sad. Now that we knew Mizushima's true feelings, all of us felt ready to accept whatever lay ahead.

Soon it was night, and the surface of the Indian Ocean sparkled with innumerable bits of luminous protozoa. Patches of ghostly phosphorescence as large as a man's hand would bob up between the waves, glide along smoothly for a time, and then disappear in the white foam that could be seen even in the dark. Some of the clusters of protozoa seemed to cling to the sides of the ship. Others followed after us; still others drifted far behind.

It looked as if the spirits of the dead were frolicking among the waves.

In the vast sky above us the stars were shining brilliantly. As the boat rolled from side to side its mast swayed through the field of stars, but to us it seemed as if the mast stood still and the stars danced around it.

We sang together softly. The sound of the waves enveloped our ship. We could almost hear the music of a harp rise out of the flying spray.

The ship sailed slowly on, day after day. Morning and evening we gazed into the clouds ahead of us, wondering how soon we would see Japan.

—THE END—

TUTTLE CLASSICS

LITERATURE 小説 (* = for sale in Japan only)

ABE, Kobo 安部公房

The Face of Another 他人の顔 ISBN 978-4-8053-0120-3*

Friends 友達 ISBN 978-4-8053-0648-2*

The Ruined Map 燃えつきた地図 ISBN 978-4-8053-0654-3*

The Woman in the Dunes 砂の女 ISBN 978-4-8053-0900-1*

AKUTAGAWA, Ryunosuke 芥川龍之介

Kappa 河童 ISBN 978-4-8053-0901-8*

Rashomon and Other Stories 羅生門 ISBN 978-4-8053-0882-0

DAZAI, Osamu 太宰治

Crackling Mountain and Other Stories 太宰治短編集 ISBN 978-0-8048-3342-4; 978-4-8053-1018-2*

No Longer Human 人間失格 ISBN 978-4-8053-1017-5*

The Setting Sun 斜陽 ISBN 978-4-8053-0672-7*

EDOGAWA, Rampo 江戸川乱歩

Japanese Tales of Mystery & Imagination 江戸川乱歩短編集 ISBN 978-0-8048-0319-9; 978-4-8053-0940-7*

ENDO, Shusaku 遠藤周作

Deep River 深い河 ISBN 978-4-8053-0618-5*

The Final Martyrs 最後の殉教者 ISBN 978-4-8053-0625-3*

Foreign Studies 留学 ISBN 978-0-8048-1626-7*

The Golden Country 黄金の国 ISBN 978-0-8048-3337-0

Scandal スキャンダル ISBN 978-4-8053-0620-8*

The Sea and Poison 海と毒薬 ISBN 978-4-8053-0330-6*

Stained Glass Elegies 遠藤周作短編集 ISBN 978-4-8053-0624-6*

Volcano 火山 ISBN 978-4-8053-0664-2*

When I Whistle 口笛を吹くとき ISBN 978-4-8053-0627-7*

HEARN, Lafcadio ラフカディオ・ハーン(小泉八雲)

Glimpses of Unfamiliar Japan 知られぬ日本の面影 ISBN 978-4-8053-1025-0

In Ghostly Japan 霊の日本 ISBN 978-0-8048-3661-6; 978-4-8053-0749-6*

Kokoro 心 ISBN 978-4-8053-1138-7; 978-4-8053-0748-9*

Kwaidan 怪談 ISBN 978-0-8048-3662-3; 978-4-8053-0750-2*

Lafcadio Hearn's Japan 小泉八雲の日本 ISBN 978-4-8053-0873-8

KAWABATA, Yasunari 川端康成

The Izu Dancer and Other Stories 伊豆の踊り子、他 ISBN 978-4-8053-0744-1*

The Master of Go 名人 ISBN 978-4-8053-0673-4*

The Old Capital 古都 ISBN 978-4-8053-0972-8*

Snow Country 雪国 ISBN 978-4-8053-0635-2*

Thousand Cranes 千羽鶴 ISBN 978-4-8053-0971-1*

MISHIMA, Yukio 三島由紀夫
After the Banquet 宴のあと ISBN 978-4-8053-0968-1*
Confessions of a Mask 仮面の告白 ISBN 978-4-8053-0232-3*
Death in Midsummer and Other Stories 真夏の死、他 ISBN 978-4-8053-0617-8*
The Decay of the Angel 天人五衰 ISBN 978-4-8053-0385-6 *
Five Modern Noh Plays 近代能楽集 ISBN 978-4-8053-1032-8*
Madame de Sade サド侯爵夫人 ISBN 978-4-8053-0659-8*
Runaway Horses 奔馬 ISBN 978-4-8053-0969-8*
Spring Snow 春の雪 ISBN 978-4-8053-0970-4*
The Temple of the Golden Pavilion 金閣寺 ISBN 978-4-8053-0637-6*
NATSUME, Soseki 夏目漱石
And Then それから ISBN 978-4-8053-1141-7
Botchan 坊ちゃん ISBN 978-0-8048-3703-3; 978-4-8053-0802-8*
Grass on the Wayside 道草 ISBN 978-4-8053-0258-3*
The Heredity of Taste 趣味の遺伝 ISBN 978-4-8053-0766-3*
I am a Cat 吾輩は猫である ISBN 978-0-8048-3265-6; 978-4-8053-1097-7*
Kokoro こころ ISBN 978-4-8053-0746-5*
Light and Darkness 明暗 ISBN 978-4-8053-0652-9 *
The Miner 坑夫 ISBN 978-4-8053-0616-1*
My Individualism and the Philosophical Foundations of Literature
私の個人主義、文芸の哲学的基礎 ISBN 978-0-8048-3603-6; 978-4-8053-0767-0*
Spring Miscellany and London Essays 永日小品 ISBN 978-0-8048-3326-4
The Three-Cornered World 草枕 ISBN 978-4-8053-0201-9
To The Spring Equinox and Beyond 彼岸過迄 ISBN 978-0-8048-3328-8;
978-4-8053-0741-0*
Tower of London 倫敦塔 ISBN 978-4-8053-0860-8*
The Wayfarer 行人 ISBN 978-4-8053-0204-0*
OE, Kenzaburo 大江健三郎
A Personal Matter 個人的な体験 ISBN 978-4-8053-0641-3*
TSUBOI, Sakae 壷井栄
Twenty-four Eyes 二十四の瞳 ISBN 978-4-8053-0772-4*
TANIZAKI, Junichiro 谷崎潤一郎
Diary of a Mad Old Man 瘋癲老人日記 ISBN 978-4-8053-0675-8*
In Praise of Shadows 陰翳礼賛 ISBN 978-4-8053-0665-9*
The Key 鍵 ISBN 978-4-8053-0632-1*
The Makioka Sisters 細雪 ISBN 978-4-8053-1189-9*
Naomi 痴人の愛 ISBN 978-0-8048-1520-8; 978-4-8053-0622-2*
The Secret History of the Lord of Musashi and Arrowroot 武州公秘話、吉野葛
ISBN 978-4-8053-0657-4*
Seven Japanese Tales 谷崎潤一郎短編集 ISBN 978-4-8054-1016-8*
Some Prefer Nettles 蓼喰う虫 ISBN 978-4-8055-0633-8*
YOSHIKAWA, Eiji 吉川英治
The Heike Story 新平家物語 ISBN 978-0-8048-3318-9; 978-4-8053-1044-1*

JAPANESE CLASSICS 古典

IHARA, Saikaku 井原西鶴

Comrade Loves of the Samurai 男色大鏡 ISBN 978-4-8053-0771-7

Five Women Who Loved Love 好色五人女 ISBN 978-0-8048-0184-3

This Scheming World 世間胸算用 ISBN 978-0-8048-3339-4; 978-4-8053-0643-7*

KAMONO, Chomei 鴨長明

The Ten Foot Square Hut and Tales of Heike 方丈記、平家物語

ISBN 978-0-8048-3676-0; 978-4-8053-0795-3*

KINO, Tsurayuki 紀貫之

The Tosa Diary 土佐日記 ISBN 978-0-8048-3695-1; 978-4-8053-0754-0*

Mother of Michitsuna 菅原道綱の母

The Gossamer Years 蜻蛉日記 ISBN 978-0-8048-1123-1

MURASAKI Shikibu 紫式部

WALEY, Arthur (trans.) The Tale of Genji 源氏物語 ISBN 978-4-8053-1081-6

SEIDENSTICKER, Edward G. (trans.) The Tale of Genji (2 Volumes)

源氏物語(2巻組) ISBN 978-4-8053-0921-6*

SUEMATSU, Kencho (trans.) The Tale of Genji 源氏物語

ISBN 978-0-8048-3823-8; 978-4-8053-0872-1*

PUETTE, William J. The Tale of Genji: A Reader's Guide 源氏物語読本

ISBN 978-4-8053-1084-7

Sei Shonagon 清少納言

The Pillow Book of Sei Shonagon 枕草子 ISBN 978-4-8053-1108-0

YOSHIDA, Kenko 吉田兼好 Essays in Idleness 徒然草 ISBN 978-4-8053-0631-4*

JAPANESE HISTORY 日本の歴史

ASTON, W. G. (trans.) Nihongi 日本書紀 ISBN 978-0-8048-3674-6; 978-4-8053-1020-5*

DUNN, Charles J.

Everyday Life in Traditional Japan 江戸の暮らし ISBN 978-4-8053-1005-2

HALL, John Whitney Japan: From Prehistory to Modern Times

日本の歴史:古代から現代まで ISBN 978-4-8053-0661-1*

KERR, George

Okinawa: The History of an Island People 沖縄の歴史 ISBN 978-0-8048-2087-5

LONGSTREET, Stephen and Ethel Yoshiwara ISBN 978-4-8053-1027-4

MASON, R.H.P. and CAIGER, J.G. A History of Japan 日本の歴史

ISBN 978-0-8048-2097-4; 978-4-8053-0792-2*

MCCULLOUGH, Helen Craig The Taiheiki: A Chronicle of Medieval Japan

太平記 ISBN 978-0-8048-3538-1; 978-4-8053-1010-6*

SANSOM, George B.

Japan: A Short Cultural History 日本文化の歴史 ISBN 978-4-8053-0874-5*

SEIDENSTICKER, Edward G.

Tokyo: From Edo to Showa 1867-1989 ISBN 978-4-8053-1024-3

TSUDA, Noritake 津田敬武 A History of Japanese Art 日本の美術史

ISBN 978-4-8053-1031-1

The Tuttle Story: "Books to Span the East and West"

Most people are surprised when they learn that the world's largest publisher of books on Asia had its beginnings in the tiny American state of Vermont. The company's founder, Charles Tuttle, came from a New England family steeped in publishing, and his first love was books—especially old and rare editions.

Tuttle's father was a noted antiquarian dealer in Rutland, Vermont. Young Charles honed his knowledge of the trade working in the family bookstore, and later in the rare books section of Columbia University Library. His passion for beautiful books—old and new—never wavered through his long career as a bookseller and publisher.

After graduating from Harvard, Tuttle enlisted in the military and in 1945 was sent to Tokyo to work on General Douglas MacArthur's staff. He was tasked with helping to revive the Japanese publishing industry, which had been utterly devastated by the war. After his tour of duty was completed, he left the military, married a talented and beautiful singer, Reiko Chiba, and in 1948 began several successful business ventures.

To his astonishment, Tuttle discovered that postwar Tokyo was actually a book-lover's paradise. He befriended dealers in the Kanda district and began supplying rare Japanese editions to American libraries. He also imported American books to sell to the thousands of GIs stationed in Japan. By 1949, Tuttle's business was thriving, and he opened Tokyo's very first English-language bookstore in the Takashimaya Department Store in Ginza, to great success. Two years later, he began publishing books to fulfill the growing interest of foreigners in all things Asian.

Though a westerner, Charles Tuttle was hugely instrumental in bringing knowledge of Japan and Asia to a world hungry for information about the East. By the time of his death in 1993, he had published over 6,000 books on Asian culture, history and art—a legacy honored by Emperor Hirohito in 1983 with the "Order of the Sacred Treasure," the highest honor Japan bestows upon non-Japanese.

The Tuttle company today maintains an active backlist of some 1,500 titles, many of which have been continuously in print since the 1950s and 1960s—a great testament to Charles Tuttle's skill as a publisher. More than 60 years after its founding, Tuttle Publishing is as active today as at any time in its history, still inspired by Charles' core mission—to publish fine books to span the East and West and provide a greater understanding of each.